The Lost

Dome of Atron

by

Barbara Moon

Table of Contents

Dedication

I dedicate this book to my dear friend, Debbie Sellmann, who so unselfishly gave of her time to edit my story thoroughly. I gleaned much from her skills and suggestions. Debbie, through the years we have known each other, you have been one of my greatest sources of encouragement.

Thanks

I want to thank my daughter, Jodi, her husband, Rick and my daughter in law, Chris, for their input and suggestions upon reading the manuscript. Thanks, Guys! You made it so much richer. I cannot do any writing project without my son, Bob. Thanks, Bob, for all your help—from rescuing my documents when the computer freezes to patiently bringing it all together at the end. I love and thank you guys.

Characters

THE UNIDANS:

The Present:

Candra, Daughter of Handen and Esleda, sister to Nathan

Gran (Karand), Mother of Handen, widow of Wilden

Lornen, friend of Gran

The Unidan Participants/Scouts in Part Three:

Women—Marland, Joden and Jaren

Men—Chregg, Richen, Borg & Jored

Ancestors of Candra:

Sandlen, Mother of Gran, wife of Jazen

Kolen, Father of Sandlen, husband to Elezaban

Damond, Father of Kolen,

Vandlyn, Father of Damond

THE TOLDENS

Eric, Second Prince of Tolden, son of evil King Krall, twin to First Prince, Stephad

Brinid, Unknown lineage

Tylina, Eric's childhood nurse

Map of Atron

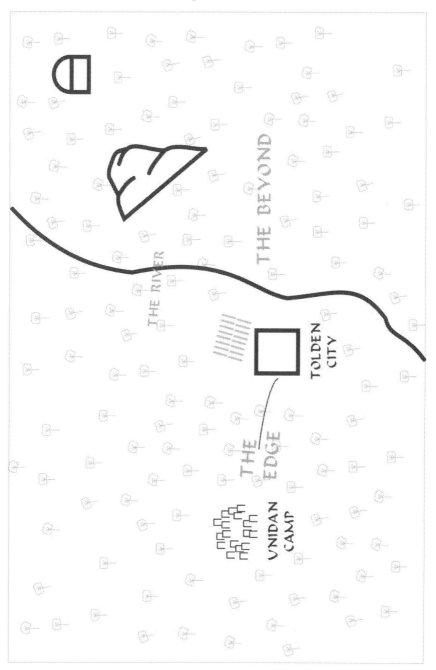

Other Books by Barbara Moon

www.lulu.com/barbaramoon   www.amazon.com

The Genesis of Atron-Book Two

The Redemption of Atron-Book Three

Joy-Filled Relationships

Handbook to Joy-Filled Parenting

Workbook for Handbook to Joy-Filled Parenting

Workbook and Guide for Hinds' Feet on High Places

Leader's Guide for Hinds' Feet on High Places'

Workbook and Guide for The Rest of the Gospel

Leader's Guide for The Rest of the Gospel

Jewels for My Journey

Jesus Never Fails

The Craziosity Twins

Part One: The People of Atron

CHAPTER ONE

Candra walked swiftly, but quietly through the early awakening forest. Her long dark hair was braided and secured in a leather band and covered with the hood of her cloak that scarcely revealed her sky-blue eyes, intent on surveying the surroundings. As a daughter of Unidan, living in the forest was all she had known and she felt at home under the sheltering trees. Like their human counterpart, the animals and birds of the forest were exceptionally quiet this morning. Candra was accustomed to hearing their squawks and smelling the odors of rotting wood, but these days she could not draw comfort from the familiar sights and smells. Atron was dying. The climate where she lived, though mild and pleasant most of the year, had not seen rain for over a year, and the Unidans were relying more and more heavily on the grain smuggled from the neighboring kingdom of Tolden. Since the only large river was in their sector, the Toldens had means to irrigate, but their cruel king had no intentions of sharing the grain that he used Unidan slaves to harvest. Smuggling grain was the only way for Unidans to have a taste of bread at their meals during this long drought.

The drought was also beginning to affect the forest creatures. More animals were leaving the area with each passing day. Good hunting was now scarce. Gardens tended around the tents of Unidan were filled with scraggly plants that barely filled a cooking pot when there was not meat. The cruel king of Tolden had posted more guards around the city. As a result, Unidan runners often brought no more than one sack of grain from each journey into

The Edge, the place that marked boundaries between Unidan and Tolden. This newest crisis placed an even greater demand on Candra's skills to safely find and meet today's runner. Dawn and twilight were the safest times to venture into The Edge. The territory between the Unidan camp and the city of Tolden could be an extremely dangerous place for either of the peoples to be. Candra's heart raced as her feet quietly brushed the dewy grass and her eyes continually darted to and fro scrutinizing the area ahead. One never knew for certain if the runner might turn out to be a Tolden. Her best safeguard was to watch for the secret, unmistakable signals given only to the Unidan runners. For safety's sake, each trek to The Edge required a new signal. The runner from Unidan passed along the next signal to the runner from Tolden when they exchanged their goods.

Today Candra's task upon entering The Edge would be two-fold. She had been asked to meet her father's runner and take, not only the grain bag, but also an important message scroll to be carried back to her father who was waiting for her at the camp. A small movement off to the side caught the corner of Candra's eye. She increased her level of caution, each foot moving more and more slowly, Tazor drawn quietly and quickly from its sheath. Shielding herself behind a large tree, Candra surveyed the territory ahead, carefully looking for today's signal. This run it was to be a blue rag. There. On that low bush about twenty steps to her left. The blue scarf hung low on the bush, limp in the quiet morning, signaling to any Unidan messenger that the runner could safely move ahead. The one who left it would have carefully scouted the area before leaving the rag. He stepped out from his hiding place as soon as he heard Candra's soft whistle. Candra slid the rolled up scroll he handed her into a deep pocket of her cape and shouldered the bulky grain bag. "May The One have His Way," she spoke softly. "May it be soon," her contact replied as they quickly parted.

Exchanging the familiar blessing triggered Candra's thoughts of Gran. Gran, her father's mother, was an important Elder on the council and knew better than anyone the old stories of Atron when everyone was united under The One. The people of Tolden no longer cared about the division and had long ago forgotten the reasons for it, as well as forgetting The One. Gran's lifelong dream had been to reunite the people of Unidan and Tolden. Unidans saw it as their Cause and each Unidan was committed to giving his or her life for the Cause.

In her mind, Candra pictured her grandmother's lovely wrinkled face framed by soft white hair, wound into a bun on the back of her head. Gran's face was marked with peace and her eyes shone with kindness, but at times she would grow sad when she spoke of the Cause. Wrapped carefully in soft skins and stored in a chest in a corner of Gran's tent was a piece of Atron's past. Gran believed it was part of the answer to reuniting Atron. She also believed it held the answer to bringing the rains again to their dying planet. That piece of the past was a very old parchment made of some kind of material unfamiliar to the Elders. The parchment was covered with strange drawings and writings and appeared to be some kind of map. Gran's hope was that it might be a map to the lost Dome of Atron's ancestors. The old stories spoke of the Dome and what it contained—Ancient books from The One as well as explanations of the origin of Atron. Perhaps the Dome would have some information about how to end the drought blighting the countryside. Never had there been such a mysterious lack of rainfall.

The parchment had been passed to Gran for over three generations from her mother's father, Kolen. Kolen was a descendant of one of Atron's early kings. Whenever Gran took out the parchment to look at it, she always pointed to a place where part of the parchment was missing. That edge was jagged and torn. This was the problem that kept the Unidans from searching for the lost Dome. Without the missing part of the parchment, it would be impossible to find the Dome. No one knew even where to begin.

The missing parchment and the lost Dome were not the only mysteries that Gran heard about as she grew up hearing the old stories. Her Elders told about something they called an electrokey that was needed to open the Dome, but the place of its keeping had also become lost to them. The hope was that finding the other half of the parchment could solve these mysteries and make The Cause of uniting the Unidan and Tolden peoples an actual event instead of just a dream.

Gran and Candra often talked about the dream of reuniting the two kingdoms that used to live side by side without conflict, until that time many years ago when Atron's two kings had a terrible disagreement. Now the people had no access to the Dome, or to their full history and The One's books that were rumored to be there in the Dome. That disagreement had brought about the division that Candra lived in today. *And no one even remembers the reasons for that old fight.* Candra said to herself. *It affects all of us. And I see how strongly Gran believes that finding the other half of her parchment would reveal the location of the electrokey and the Dome so we could reopen it and end the conflict. Could we also find a way to bring the rain again?* she mused.

Candra knew there were many other stories known to the Elders, but these stories were kept from the young people until they were older. There was no one who knew all of what had happened to the parchment or the electrokey, as through the years, some of the story had been lost in the process of passing it down through word of mouth. As Candra continued to ponder, she realized that probably no one in Tolden even knew about the old days, much less about the Books, the Dome and the parchment. *Toldens mostly know the hate that comes from that split,* thought Candra.

Gran kept her parchment safely stored, seldom removing it. There had been times in the Council meetings of the Elders that different people had tried to convince Gran to let them venture into the Beyond, the completely unknown area that surrounded both the Unidan camp and the Tolden city, without both pieces of the parchment. Everyone wanted to search for the Dome. Gran refused. It was much too dangerous and unknown, she always said. No one went out into the parts of Atron that used to be. All that remained was Tolden and Unidan. But the Cause of reuniting them was a struggle almost beyond hope without finding the Dome, and the journey would be a nightmare without the total parchment.

Gran had learned of the Cause from her mother, and now Candra took every opportunity to learn all she could about it from Gran. *One day I will be the leader when Father goes to be with the One*, she mused as her feet automatically found the hidden paths to Unidan. *What kind of world will I lead? The famine and our lack of progress with the Cause to reunite the people of Atron seem overwhelming. We must find the Dome and the Books if we are to save Atron. I do wish Gran would let us go search even without the other parchment.*

A rustle in some near-by bushes interrupted Candra's concerns for Atron. She stopped just off the path and lowered the grain sack to draw her Tazor. Her ears, well trained in the language of forest noises, strained to hear other sounds. After a few minutes, familiar sounds assured her that it was safe to continue. It was not much further now to the outer guards who would be watching and ready to meet her.

Arriving near the camp, Candra passed the heavy sack to one of the guards and hurried through rows of tents surrounding the Meeting Square. Each family had its own tent where the younger children were watched carefully over until the time they were ready to have a tent of their own next to their parents. The tents were made of hides left from the animals that had been caught for food by Unidan hunters. Each tent was squared, with a sloping roof that had been fortified by large leaves woven together to assure dryness when rain did come. A fire pit for cooking, constructed near one interior side of each tent, had a small opening in the side where smoke could exit. Most everyone filled their tents with large pillows and cushions stuffed with bird feathers and grasses that would provide comfort while sitting or sleeping. When it was chilly, cloaks and blankets, kept out the cold. As she walked through the camp, seeing the tents reminded Candra that she was home among friends and family.

How I love the people, she thought warmly, as she entered her parents' tent, and handed her father the message tube. He and her mother were sitting by the fire, quietly talking. As Candra kissed her father on his bearded cheek, she said wearily, "The days of receiving carts filled with the grain sacks seem far away, don't they, Father? And getting message tubes used to be a rare thing for us. I wish we could go back to when it was the other way around."

"You are so right, My Daughter. Did you have trouble while you were in the Edge?" questioned Handen, his large hand circling the message tube. As he looked at his daughter it was easy to see where Candra's piercing blue eyes had come from, as eyes just like them searched her face.

"No, Father. It went well." Candra turned to kiss her mother's cheek and say hello. "You know how often we've heard that the Toldens discuss our expertise with the Tazor. I think their fear of our readiness and skill helps keep them out of the Edge." Looking back to her Father, she asked, "May I know what's in the message tube? I'm ready to sit on the Council soon, am I not? I want to help more than just going as a runner. Anyone can do that."

"In many ways you are ready, yet you show impatience, My Beloved." Handen's warm smile took any sting from his words as he continued. "Your time will come. You will know what you need to know when it's time to know. Enjoy your freedom from worry yet a little longer. I will take care of this message."

"You will have many years to help the Cause, My Daughter," encouraged her mother, Esleda. "You have trained well and listened and studied. Patience is an honorable and lovely trait for a leader of our people. The One grows it in you as you practice it, trusting that it is in you because He is in you." Candra bent to hug her Mother again. Once again, she admired her mother's long brown hair. Braided and wrapped neatly around her perfect oval face, it made a lovely frame for her mother's kind brown eyes. Her beauty came from inside as well as out. Esleda was such a wise and good mother, a perfect Companion to help lead Unidan alongside Handen.

"Thank you, Mother. As always you help me remember the truths I have taken. You know that I want to grow in every way. So many things take practice by faith, don't they?" Sensing that this interview with her father had come to an end, Candra touched each parent's shoulder with a hand, and said, "I'm going to my tent to rest and then find Nathan. We'll see you both this evening."

As she turned to leave Candra noticed the furrows deepen in Handen's brow. His broad shoulders slumped noticeably as he read the message. *Father carries great responsibility*, thought Candra. *No matter how much I insist that I'm ready, Father continues to make me wait. He always says the same thing about me hearing the news whenever it's time to know it. I want to sit with the Council now instead of waiting until he's gone. Others have begun immediately after their Becoming Day, but Father won't allow me to quite yet. He says I'll hear that news also whenever it's time.* "Learning to wait is part of your training," her parents were always saying.

CHAPTER TWO

As Candra walked towards her own tent to rest from her run to the Edge, thinking about the Council reminded Candra of her Becoming Day just a month ago. Sometimes it felt like she had waited for that day forever—the day when she would become a full Participant in The Cause and take her First Companion. Other times it seemed like only yesterday that she had been a little one sitting in Gran's classes, learning to read and learning about The Cause, The One, and about Atron. Had it been so long since she had been trained in the ways of obedience, truthfulness, openness and following The One from within? *I remember well the ways of our camp with little ones*, she thought. *All the grown Unidans take time with the young ones, like they did Nathan and me, teaching us not to lie and not to hate, not to fight. There are many days of discipline while we are growing up;* she chuckled remembering some of hers, *but always with love and talk of The One. I remember when I asked The One to come inside for myself. That was a wonderful, beautiful day and I have never been quite the same. It's much easier now to hear Him and to follow Him. He's here inside me all the time, even when I'm struggling. All I have to do is turn inside and talk to Him.*

As she made some hot tea and settled herself on the cushions near her fire pit, Candra thought about Nathan her younger brother and how surprised he had been when she asked him to be her First Companion. Sipping her hot brew, a smile started to creep across Candra's face as she remembered the day she asked Nathan to be her First Companion. They had reminisced many times since about those days around her Becoming. They knew everything that each other had thought about.

The day Candra asked him to be her Companion had been a day of many surprises for Nathan. Early that morning he had tiptoed quietly into Candra's tent, and startled her awake by dripping water in her face. *Will she be different after her Becoming Day?* Nathan wondered to himself as he prepared to jump away from Candra's reach. *Will the days filled with fun and teasing suddenly become serious and dull? Well, at least not yet,* he quickly decided as his sister woke up, sputtering and yelling at him. She grabbed for his pants leg and missed, but in a flash she was out the opening running after him. She quickly grabbed his shirt and dragged him back inside her tent. Nathan laughed so hard, he found himself crying for mercy to get her to stop poking her fingers up and down his rib cage. Candra stared at her handsome brother. Even though he had two more years until his Becoming, his strength already surpassed hers, and his cunning with the Tazor increased each day. *I can think of no one in Unidan I would rather count on as my protector in battle, should that day ever come.*

"Now you must pay your debt, Nathan," she said suddenly as she sat astride his back. "You get to be my First Companion at the ceremony next week. What do you think of that?"

"Candra!" sputtered Nathan as play suddenly turned to serious discussion. "Do you mean it? I never thought---you honor me," "To be your Companion! Truly I am honored. Thank you."

"I would have it no other way until the day I am joined to my Last Companion in marriage." She smiled at the pleased look on her brother's face. "It is not often that one who is younger is called to be a Companion," Nathan said humbly. "I will not take it lightly."

Nathan's chest swelled with a deep sigh of contentment as he let it sink in and thought about what it might be like to be Candra's Companion. They had always been close as children of Unidan often were, though he sometimes found himself wishing he were the older. The teachings from his childhood helped Nathan to not dwell long upon those regrets. Instead, all the excitement from Candra's upcoming celebration had him thinking ahead toward his own Becoming Day and the things he was continually learning from The One. *The One knows best,* he thought as he shook off any stray regrets and studied the excited look on his sister's glowing face. There he read her feelings of anticipation for this special ceremony and all it would mean to her.

"You know how long I've waited for this day," her words echoed his thoughts. "No more schooling except with Gran, Father and Mother. I'll become a full Participant, capable of fighting battles and ready to search for the Dome should the parchment be found."

Candra came back to the present, shaking her head as she suddenly realized that her teacup was empty. Her mind stayed in the present long enough to go to the fire and refill her cup with scalding tea. Returning to her seat among the cushions, she drifted back to the day when her long awaited ceremony had finally arrived.

# # # #

Just like now, Candra remembered, she had been inside her tent. Instead of relaxing, she had spent her morning washing and dressing in the traditional ceremonial clothes only worn at such very special occasions. Woven by her mother, her special linen dress was made from plants that grew in the forest around Unidan. Using threads died in her own color pots, Esleda had beautifully stitched delicate patterns around both the neck and sleeves. The dress flowed to the ground, falling white and pure around Candra's feet, with long flowing sleeves that almost covered her hands.

In honor of this special morning Candra's dark hair fell to her waist, loosened from its usual braid and brushed to a high sheen. Her sparkling blue eyes reflected her joy in this day. As her mother helped her dress, they talked about Candra's younger years and laughed at how fast the time had gone. Candra's glow came not just from the excitement of this occasion, but like her mother's, sprung from a beauty that was from deep within. Esleda lovingly kissed her daughter's cheek while placing a beautiful garland created from a bouquet of delicate, pale pink and purple flowers upon her daughter's head. "I will see you next at the ceremony," she whispered in her daughter's ear before turning to leave and finish her own preparations at the Meeting Square. Though it wasn't yet clear to Esleda all that might happen to Candra as she became a full participant, Esleda was able to rest in knowing that Candra knew The One, and He lived in her. For years her daughter had listened to the Elders, especially Gran, as they taught the children each morning about the beliefs of the Unidan people. Candra was growing in the knowledge that love for all was the underlying principle that made their culture work. In a tradition that had been passed down through each generation, every Unidan was always considered special for their uniqueness, as well as for the gifts they brought to the group as a whole. Quickly examining in her mind every area of Candra's training, Esleda knew that her lovely daughter had been well prepared to enter this next season of her young life. As Esleda bent to leave the tent, Candra said softly, "Thank you, Mother. You have taught me well. I love you." Esleda's smile was answer enough.

Candra continued thinking through the lessons from her younger years. As she watched her mother leave, she knew that the lessons would now be tested in a deeper way. Her heart longed to know who her Last Companion would be. In the camp there were none that drew her interest. As she became a full participant, what would The One change so that she would find him? Her best friend, Joden had already joined her Last Companion, Richen. Joden was a few seasons older, but she and Candra had been close most of their lives. They always sat together in the classes with Gran and the other teachers and explored the forest together at ever opportunity. They still spent as much time with each other as they could find to do so. It was wonderful

          2006 Barbara Moon

to have such a good friend, one with whom she could pour out her heart like she did with Gran and her mother. Would she know a Last Companion's love or would she lead her people without knowing the love and support of a Companion? One thing she did know—the union with a Last Companion would last forever-- nothing but death could separate two who had been joined together within and without. Both people must consider taking each other as a Last Companion very seriously. In Unidan, young ones pledged at an early age to remain pure. They were taught the importance of waiting for intimacy. Only a Last Companion would know you completely. On the day of Becoming, the First Companions would pledge to help each other keep these important commitments until the coming of the Last Companion.

I know Father will remind us of these things, Candra's thoughts continued. *Relating to one another is sacred and only as we know each other through the One can we relate to each other fully. How wonderful it is to be here in Unidan. There's such love and caring among our people. Whether I serve them alone or with a Companion, I will have love either way. But I do hope The One has someone for me.* And as was usual whenever she thought about her wonderful people, she longed for the Toldens to know The One's love as well.

Gran has told me often how desperately the Toldens need to know The One. Their city is not a pleasant place to live, she says. I wonder what it would be like to meet a Tolden, Candra thought. *Not that I want to,* she quickly added. *The spies who go back and forth to live say the Toldens don't love each other and they fight all the time. Children are not cared for and their king is harsh and cruel. Without The One, we Unidans would fare no better, I'm certain,* Candra admitted. *All the more reason to help them some day when the Elders say it is time.*

Candra stood at the opening of her tent, not wanting to wrinkle her Becoming dress as she waited for the call to come to the Meeting Square. Her thoughts turned to yesterday when she had visited Gran on her last day as a child. "I'm frightened about tomorrow," Candra had told Gran, while her grandmother gently brushed the tangles out of her freshly washed hair. "But I am excited as well," she continued. "I have waited and trained for this day for a long time."

"Yes, you have, My Child," Gran agreed. "Our children begin their training at a young age. You learned to read, you studied our people's history with the Elders and practiced long hours with your Tazor. As the younger ones came along you helped them learn." Gran paused as she considered all the training that Unidan children go through. "The part of our training that I love the most," she continued with a smile at Candra, "is how families and all of us together take a vital role in training young ones' to know The One Within. Knowing and taking Him inside are the basis of our life. Knowing Him and His ways helps prepare us to fully understand the Cause and how to live by The One's own life and power." As Gran finished brushing Candra's fresh smelling hair, she put down the brush and looked into her granddaughter's smiling face. "And I will say that you have trained well, My Daughter!"

"Thank you, Gran. It is much of your doing and I love every moment of being with you." Another radiant smile crept across Candra's face as she leaned to give her grandmother a big hug. As they drew apart, Candra asked a question that she had asked many, many times before, "Would you tell me again of your Becoming Day, Gran?"

"With pleasure, My Love." Gran warmed to the invitation to relive one of her favorite memories. "It was one of the most memorable days of my life, as it is one of the most important for all Unidan young ones. My day was sunny and clear, as will be yours tomorrow. Like you, I could hardly wait for the ceremony to begin. Such an important day--the day you become your own--and at one and the same time a greater part of the whole. This day signals the time for putting into practice all that you have learned and will continue to learn and understand deep inside yourself."

Candra, nodded in agreement. "All ages of children are very important in our camp, aren't they, Gran? But I sense there's something really special about Becoming. Each year as we grow we receive a little more responsibility and freedom. Tomorrow I participate in a ceremony that symbolizes my completion of childhood training, though I realize that I will still be subject to the Council's decisions."

"Yes, as you say, Love, you are part of the whole of our camp and none of us will ever be totally independent from The One. Though you are well prepared, I think becoming a Participant will not be as easy for you as you think. Yet you have The One, and you will continue to grow even more as you know Him better.

You've practiced your lessons until your skills with the Tazor have become quite adequate, and the time you are going to spend with your First Companion will help sharpen you for your future uniting with your Last Companion. There will be both joys and sorrows after your ceremony tomorrow. There will also be deepening lessons, and though you will have others to look to for comfort, you will truly be learning for yourself as never before."

"Gran, though I have listened to you many times, I cannot see these things of which you speak. In my heart I want to hurry forward, finish this Cause that we've committed ourselves to for so long, and find out who it is that will become my Last Companion. Some days I feel the pull to stay here with you and Father and Mother where it is safe, but then other days I feel ready to go and take my place. Was it like that for you?"

Gran thoughtfully put the brush away and continued telling her story. "As I remember it was much the same for me, My Child. I had many of the same fears and unanswerable questions you describe, the same anticipation and jubilation over the changes to come, and yet at the same time, the surety of what I knew to be true. Without guidance from The One Within, this bridge from childhood to the grown-up world would have been much more difficult for me to cross."

"I understand from what I've heard that this journey you are taking is not the same in Tolden as it is here. While our children move from one phase of life to the next with longing and growing confidence, the young ones who live there become wild and destructive as they approach the time when they should become builders and creators and keepers of their people. It's not the Tolden's way to learn the One Within. Their fears and the new feelings that come with the move into adulthood cannot be taken to Him for wisdom and insight. Here, everyone works together like parts of a whole, while there they are more like our great stream when it used to flood—with no banks to guide them down the right channel. Because they are so wild and destructive, they flood and destroy everything in sight. Growing up in Unidan, gives you a great advantage over the young ones of Tolden."

"Gran, what understanding I have of myself this day, at the place I am, is because of all I have learned from The One, who is continually giving meaning and purpose to my life. Since my youth He has spoken to me in my heart, and as I have been taught, I have taken all my questions and longings to Him. Though I know Him not yet as well as you do, I am constantly learning. This I've learned: He shall calm my fears and be my patience in my longings so that I'll be able to wait for His answers."

"Yes, Dear One, that is most important--to know yourself by seeing yourself through His eyes. It is the only way to truly know yourself and grow into all He means for you. Although here in Unidan we have found the way to have peace with one another, there still often comes a temptation to know yourself only by looking through another person's eyes. Of course, we see ourselves through others' eyes and yet at the same time while leaning on each other for encouragement is our way with one another, there will always be times when we fail one another. The One, however, never fails us and is always there to guide and encourage us in the way we should go."

"I know what you say is the truth, Gran, and I will try not to look only to another to truly know and understand myself. Relying on The One makes all the difference, doesn't it?" As Candra continued to skillfully rebraid her hair, she peppered her grandmother with more questions, forgetting for the moment her original request to hear more of Gran's Becoming Day.

"The Cause is vital to our people's survival, isn't it? There is so much strife between our people and the Toldens. Atron must be reunited before we all can live in peace. The drought and the lack of food or water, make it so important that we find the Dome and the Ancient Books to help us learn how to restore the rain." Candra was close to tears, and as she talked, her frustration and desire to see changes in her world seemed almost too much to bear. "Why do the people of Tolden not see how much we need each other? The runners who go there bring back stories about the suffering of the people who live in Tolden and of the hostilities that continue to grow towards us. The people there seem to want none of The One. We hear the awful stories about how cruelly the king of Tolden treats his subjects."

Looking over at her grandmother, Candra asked tearfully, "Gran, remember when Borg told us about the time he was a runner for grain and he saw one of the Tolden soldiers beating a Tolden worker from the fields? The poor man was bleeding and almost could not get up. The soldier drug him back into the fields and made him start working again, shouting at him that he could have water when it was time for water."

"Oh yes, my dear, I remember that story from Borg--and the one about the children that were begging by the king's gate because they were so hungry. The king himself came to the top of the wall and poured a bucket of garbage scraps onto the children's heads, laughing and yelling at them to enjoy the meal and get away from his castle."

"And I don't even want to talk about what he does to Unidans that are captured and taken there," Candra agonized. All that we hear tells us that there is much unrest among his people as a result of the atrocities he has committed against our Unidans and his own people." Blinking the tears away, Candra looked into her grandmother's compassionate eyes, pleading, "I wish I could go and tell them all how unnecessary their suffering really is." Grabbing Gran's soft, wrinkly hands with her own she asked earnestly, "Why, Gran? Why do they not see?"

"They cannot, Little One. The Toldens do not seek because they do not believe--they do not believe because they do not seek. They think our stories are untrue and they are unwilling to seek for answers. They have forgotten the days when Atron was united, when the First Kings worked together and the Ancient Books were read and followed by all. They cannot remember how it was before the great Dome of Atron was lost to us, when everyone lived in peace and there was plenty for all."

"Gran, do you think we'll ever find the electrokey and the Dome? From the many times we've talked about it, I can feel how much you desire this."

"You know, Candra, we still have only half the parchment that will lead us to the Dome. Until we find the lost half we don't know where to start. No one on the Council even remembers exactly in which direction we could begin to seek. The forests are vast and many rumors remain of the dangers for those who venture out into the Beyond. Of this I'm sure, finding the Dome and the Ancient Books would give us the information we will need to bring the rain and help reunite Atron." Gran's face grew sad as she thought about the many years she had been waiting to see the fulfillment of her life long dream. Her voice filled with resolve, "The other parchment, if it has not been destroyed, must be somewhere in Tolden. Yet from what I can gather from the information our runners bring to us, the people there are told, in one way or another, that there is no One and no Dome. How could the parchment mean anything to them even if they did know about it? And now, with many people becoming desperate for food as the drought continues, there may be no Atron to reunite unless The One brings us the other half of the parchment soon."

"I am ready to go into the forest, into the very Beyond if necessary, when we have the parchments!" Candra fervently exclaimed. "I would go now without the parchment if the Council would allow it. I know Nathan would go with me! We wouldn't fear the dangers of the unknown. Don't they see that we must somehow bring the rain soon? With the Ancient Books and the knowledge they contain, we could give the hope of The One to all of Atron. The people of Tolden suffer so much at the hand of their cruel king. He and his heirs must be removed. Then there could be true peace among us, with no more raids . . . and The Edge gone forever!"

"I hear your passion for our Cause, My Daughter, and I love that it is so strong in your heart. But we must continue to wait for The One's perfect timing. He will have His way." Gran looked into her granddaughter's eyes, knowing well the intensity of that desire to find the Dome.

"Remember the story I've told you about my trek to find the Dome without the map?" Gran reminded Candra softly.

"Yes, I do remember your lessen with Lornen, Gran," Candra replied humbly. "It's one of my favorite stories, but I forget it sometimes when my passion overtakes me. Thank you for reminding me." Smiling at her Gran, she added, "I come by it honestly, don't I?"

"Yes, you do, Dear One— and your love of hearing truth as well." Gran's smile reflected Candra's.

"Now," Gran said, changing the subject, "it seems to me that you were asking to hear more about my Becoming Day. Is that not correct?"

"Yes! Please, tell me again about your dress, Gran. I love it when you tell that part and show me your dress that you keep so neatly folded away in your trunk."

Gran's face lit up brightly as her mind returned to the excitement that had surrounded her own Becoming Day. Candra could see in Gran's eyes how much she cherished the memory. "Like your mother has done for you, my mother, Sandlen, made my dress. It was also white, but the sleeves were stitched in the color of green that you see in our forest. Down the front ran two rows of yellow flowers, intricately stitched to match the band of yellow flowers in my hair. How well I remember walking from my tent to go to the square! There were four of us waiting for our Becoming ceremony, each of us standing with our First Companions. All the people were waiting for us in the square. Your Great grandfather, Jazen, with Sandlen by his side, so poised, so tall, stood ready to welcome and commission us. This tradition has been passed down for many generations, so what was said to me then will be much the same at your ceremony tomorrow."

Gran paused for a moment to stir the fire and put on a fresh pot of water for tea. Candra watched and waited until Gran continued, "I had asked Lornen to be my First Companion. We had always been very close, but did not feel the love of the One between us for becoming Last Companions. Our commitment was strong and would be proven, first in the Raids and then when your Grandfather, Wilden, came to ask me to be his Last Companion. But that, of course, is another story," Gran finished with a chuckle. Leaning over to touch Candra's hand, she added, "and I know that your day will be just as wonderful." Taking the now steaming pot from the fire, Gran poured its contents into two small bowls, offering one to Candra. They sat together quietly and drank their tea enjoying each other's company for just a few more minutes on Candra's last day as a child.

CHAPTER THREE

Candra took the last sip of her tea and slowly put her cup down as her thoughts returned to the present. It had now been a month since her big day. *I can't seem to keep my mind in the here and now*, she thought ruefully. She enjoyed reliving all that had happened on her Becoming Day. *Now, where was I?* she thought, and brought her mind back to the moment right after her mother had left the tent to make her preparations for the celebration in the square. Once her mother was gone, Candra had gone to find Nathan, interrupting him as he stood looking into his mirror glass, lost in his thoughts. Quietly, she watched his fingers unconsciously comb through his thick brown hair until it shone. Candra glanced at her brother's face, wondering about its seriousness. *What are you thinking about, my brother?* She wasn't far off with her silent guess that Nathan, too, was thinking of the coming ceremony and what it would mean for his life as Candra's First Companion. He couldn't help but marvel at the turn of events that had simultaneously given him new serious responsibilities and at the same time opened up the very real possibility of danger involved with the assignments that might come as a Participant and First Companion. Taking one of the soft, richly textured ceremonial robes worn by all the other First Companions in his family, Nathan reverently pulled it over his shoulders. He felt a rise of fear as he pulled the robe around him, but pushed the fear away as he quickly turned to The One as his peace. *Being chosen as a First Companion makes me an official Participant in the Cause, even though I've yet passed only sixteen summers.* He knew the responsibilities such an honor would carry. A little uncertain about whether he was ready to meet this new challenge, he turned to The One for guidance and reassurance. *The One knows what's best and is always in me. I rest in that knowing. Wherever Candra goes, I will go until she finds her Last . . . .*

Finding it difficult to remain silent any longer, Candra interrupted Nathan, pulling on his robe. "Nathan! Come on. Quit dreaming. Today is the day! We need to reaffirm our pledge alone, here, before we can go,"

"Candra, you startled me," Nathan grinned at his sister. Then his eyes growing serious again, he said softly, "It's all been spinning around in my head--our part in our Cause, Gran's words, finding the Ancient Books and the Dome, what is happening today.

Thanks for bringing me back so we can finish our preparations. I feel a little scared when I think about the responsibilities that will come with being your Companion. There have been few skirmishes lately with the Toldens-- when the runners have freed some of the field workers, but Father and the Council speak of things becoming worse. There has even been talk of a Raid."

"I know," Candra nodded, remembering. "The last Council meeting was heated with debates sparked from just what you've been saying. From the reports coming in from runners, the Elders feel that King Krall's reign may be nearing its end and they are also thinking that Prince Stephad has already shown by his actions that his reign could be much worse than what we've already seen. Rumors are circulating that talk about how he is totally unsympathetic toward the Cause and even encourages the continued disunity of Atron, even wishing it to grow stronger, to the point of having none of our people around at all--except as slaves."

Hearing this news from his sister sobered Nathan even more. He gazed steadily into Candra's eyes, choosing his words very carefully. "Much may be required of us very soon. We both have been waiting for the time when we could help our people. It may well be coming very soon. I'm ready to exchange the First Companion's pledge with you." He paused long enough to calm his heart and then began speaking in a clear, strong voice," Candra, I promise to do my best to protect you in battle; to sacrifice myself for your good if necessary; to speak with truth to you at all times; and to practice with you the qualities we want to learn to have in order to live closely with another."

"And I pledge to you, Nathan, that I will also protect you in battle; that I will be a willing sacrifice for you when you most need it; that I will speak the truth, listen to your admonitions, and practice the openness necessary to live more closely with another." Hugging her brother, Candra smiled, "Do you think we are ready to go before the people and the Elders?"

"We're ready, Candra," he answered humbly. "I am honored to be your First Companion."

# # # #

All of Unidan had gathered at the platform in the Meeting Square to be a part of today's ceremony honoring the new Participants. The platform was made of polished wood and stood proudly in the center of the square. It rose waist high and was large enough for ten people to stand on and been seen by the crowd. Today, as for other special events, the ground around the platform was strewn with large white flowers while the edges of the platform were lined with every color of flowers that grew in Unidan. As she approached, Candra's eyes looked lovingly at each face in the crowd of people, leisurely talking with each other as they waited for the event to begin. As the people saw Candra approach, they grew quiet and parted, making a way for her to walk through to the platform. She smiled and nodded at most of them, thinking to herself, *of course they are making a path for me now. They're the ones who have always helped me make it through. Everyone in the camp is a special part of my life.*

Though many years had passed since Atron had been divided through the anger of the First Kings, the Unidan camp was still rather small, and purposefully so. Children were not brought into the world lightly. Each one would be important to the camp and to The One. Parents wished to have plenty of time for loving and training them in His ways, so growth in Unidan happened very slowly. As Candra's parents, Handen and Esleda's happiness on this special day stemmed from the work, love and training they had given in order that they might see their lovely daughter reach this day and become a Participant.

Now walking among the people, Candra glanced up at her father and saw his face full of pride, and his eyes unusually shiny. As Atron's leader, Handen had presided over many of the young ones' Becoming Days, but this one felt almost overwhelming. Esleda, not quite as good at hiding her own tears of joy, gracefully dabbed her eyes with a soft cloth. The people, watching the parents with their daughter, couldn't help but see the love and pride that flowed between them. As he watched his daughter nearing the platform, Handen thought about all the discussions they had had through the years. He knew she was ready for this next step that would eventually bring her to leadership of this small, but amazing group of people who stood with him this day. He knew that Candra had learned from many hours with her mother, as Esleda prepared her for life to come with her Last Companion. And Gran as well--Candra had learned much about The One and of the old days from Gran. She would be a good leader when it came to be her time.

Candra eagerly hurried up the steps, with Nathan exactly one pace behind her. Clothed in white, they stood quietly beside Handen and Esleda. "This, My People, is the Becoming Day for our daughter, Candra," their father began with a smile. "Her training is complete, her character proven. She has chosen for her First Companion, her brother, Nathan. Continuing the custom of our people, he will stand with her until that day of her uniting with her Last Companion. Should she not have a Last Companion before Nathan's Becoming Day, she will stand with him."

Turning to look at his beautiful daughter, Handen began, "Candra, today begins your eighteenth season and as such it is the day that we recognize your official dedication to the Cause. It is the day we declare that you are an adult, ready for new responsibilities as well as freedoms as you serve The One and the people of Atron. On this day, you take your First Companion as your next step in preparing for the one who will be your Last Companion. Nathan will remind you of The One's truth when you are confused or forget and will come along side you to help when you encounter struggles and problems. Today you are also renewing your childhood pledge to hold yourself, your body, in purity, keeping that part of you sacred and pure to be shared only with your Last Companion."

With a loving look, Handen began the vows with Candra. "Having exchanged in private these vows with your First Companion, do you, Candra pledge these oaths the Ancients have written regarding your personal journey? Will you commit yourself to the Cause of reuniting Atron, and do everything asked of you to help find the Dome and recover the Ancient Books should that opportunity come about within your lifetime?"

"Yes, Father, I give my pledge to all you have said."

Turning next to his son, Handen asked, "Do you, Nathan, pledge to stand with Candra in battle, to be willing to sacrifice yourself for her, to speak to her of Truth and to encourage her in openness as she continues to prepare for her Last Companion?"

"I, too, Father, give my pledge to all you have said."

"Now, people of Unidan, having heard these pledges, return your own pledge of support and love." The people shouted and cheered as one for the new Participants as they turned to walk back down the platform steps. The serious part of the ceremony came to an end and the celebrating began with eating, music and dancing. Friends and family gathered around the new Participants, hugging and wishing them well. Later as the crowd around her thinned, Candra's eyes caught Gran watching her with a smile of satisfaction on her face. Candra ran into her grandmother's warm embrace.

CHAPTER FOUR

Brinid traveled alone. It was the safest way. There was no one else to look after--or depend on to look out for her. Her faded cloak covered a rough shirt and ragged pants. Her boots were so scuffed that it was almost impossible to see their color. When Brinid pulled the cloak's ragged hood around her hair and face, she could easily be mistaken for a boy. That was just fine with her. She had all of her possessions, everything she owned, painstakingly packed in her knapsack. She carried it slung over her shoulder under her cloak, fiercely guarding it at all times. She hid her Sedat in her left boot, placed there for quick and easy retrieval. She was good with it, too. She had even been known to outwit others who carried Tazors. The Sedat, a small, sharp knife-like weapon, fit her well because she was small and deft. Her strength was deceiving and often gave her an advantage when others underestimated her skill.

Tolden is such a horrible place to live, Brinid thought. She could hear people bickering and shouting at each other as they shoved their way through the crowded, dirty streets. The increasing lack of food had put people in a foul and desperate humor, making the market a dangerous place to be. Life in the city had always been hard, even for one with a family. King Krall spent most of his time consumed with keeping the Unidan influence out of the city, instead of focusing on the needs of his people. And he certainly did not help loners like Brinid, who walked the streets, having no one to go home to, and no place to call home.

The King and his court, *the privileged ones,* many called them, had yet to feel the extent of the near-famine conditions that people outside the castle faced every day. That left little indeed for the invisible ones like Brinid, who had a big problem just finding leftovers in the trash or food that was easy to steal. Garbage certainly had never been her favorite meal. She much preferred to find fresh food when she scouted the stands in the market, or to have a decent meal bought with another's money she had managed to pilfer.

The days of finding fresh food that had been left on the ground to rot, were now long gone. With food so scarce, every shopkeeper watched his inventory with a keen eye. Very little would escape his notice. And even one skilled at being invisible, as Brinid had trained herself to be, had to be very careful.

The constant search to fill her grumbling stomach with food and to find a place to lay her head at night would have been enough for Brinid to worry about, but she also had another very big problem: her continuing hatred of The Unidans. When she had asked why she was alone, left to roam the streets of Tolden, others had explained that her parents were killed in one of the long-ago raids when she was still very young.

She hated the Unidans for depriving her of her family. The stealing, hiding, and fighting she had done all her life: they were to blame. They were the reason she roamed the streets of Tolden barely surviving. Brinid hated hearing the rumors in the streets about the Unidans that told of a people that did not believe in killing or hate. Hadn't they destroyed her family? She certainly did not believe the rumors that said they could end the dreadful drought and bring all of Atron back together.

How could the Unidans, who did not even live in a city, possibly end the famine? Who were they to speak words of unity and peace? Because of them she had nothing but a life of struggle. *Ha! What could this city know of peace? If it's not in turmoil because the people are rioting, the King sends his men to stir up their own brand of chaos,* she grumbled to herself. When captive Unidans had managed to escape from the work they were forced to do in the fields of Tolden, the King would send his men to look for unattached people in the city who could take their places in the fields. Brinid already had twice been scooped up and taken to the fields--and twice escaped. She did not want to hear or speak about the scum who lived in Unidan, who had made her life so very difficult.

Her stomach growling, Sedat now drawn and hidden in her sleeve, Brinid's green eyes diligently searched the early-evening crowd for a likely victim of her stealth. She had seldom even been noticed, much less been caught on her forays into the market. *There, she thought. That man in the brown robe.* She slipped up behind him deftly cutting the strap to his bag in one quick motion. Her prize in hand, Brinid started walking through the marketplace as if nothing had happened, the Sedat returned to her boot.

Only this time, the man had felt her touch and yelled loudly. At his unexpected outburst, Brinid sped up to a run, quickly ducking into the crowd and heading around the corner of a small building. Sensing the developing uproar behind her, Brinid instinctively dove into the first dark doorway she could find. Almost hidden beneath a wooden stairwell, the small open doorway provided a welcome hiding place, so she sat down quietly. Panting but relieved by her escape, she waited for her pursuers to catch up and hopefully pass her by.

"What is it, My Child?" a voice beckoned from further inside the dimly lit room. Startled out of her quiet watchfulness, Brinid reached down with her left hand and again quickly withdrew her well-sharpened Sedat from its hiding place in her boot. Then she crouched, prepared to defend herself, and whispered urgently.

"Who's there? Answer or I am prepared to kill you!"

"You have entered my doorway unbidden. Would you then kill me in my own room?" the voice answered. "What I have is yours. What is it that you need?"

As her eyes adjusted to the shadows, Brinid glimpsed a harmless looking old man, reclining in a corner on his pallet. "I need nothing," snapped Brinid. "I take care of myself. I need nothing, or no one. I only stopped here for a second to recover. I will be going now." As Brinid stood up, she heard the old man's voice again, "My name is Lornen, Child. What is yours?"

"I do not give my name so quickly, Old Man. I have no use for friends or manners. All are out for themselves, and I most of all. Let the King's court and ones such as you exchange names. I will keep mine to myself."

"What or who has hurt you, Small One? Where comes this pain that brings such bitter words? A light shines in the darkness and a path to happiness is waiting to be found by those who seek it. The One Whose Books are Lost beckons all to come who would know their need."

"Shut up, Old Man! I'll hear no more of that talk. I've heard such gibberish whispered and rumored in many places on the streets. It is forbidden to talk such, and I will hear no more of that Unidan nonsense. There are no books and there is no shining place." Brinid turned and stooped to leave through the low doorway.

"Wait, My Son! Are you not hungry this fine evening? At least you can share a meal with me before you go. Come. Light the taper. I was just resting a little from my work, when you entered."

Lornen rose from his pallet and began to set out bread and cheese. Confused by this sudden turn of events--someone who would willingly share his bread with her, Brinid still felt somewhat calmed by his presence. The tenseness in her shoulders relaxed as she carefully placed the Sedat back in her boot and stood up. She looked Lornen squarely in the face.

"Just leave off the garbage talk and I might decide to rest here for a little while," she growled. "Oh! And don't ask me any more nosey questions." Brinid remained cautiously on guard, watching as the old man went about laying out their simple meal. It had been a very long time since she had shared a meal with anyone other than the occasional times in a crowded pub when she had scrounged money to buy food. Her struggles with constant rejection, the hard city life and her daily adventures to find food had long ago destroyed any trust that Brinid might have in others. Never having known who she was or where she had come from, caused Brinid great shame. And her constant struggles to keep herself fed, sometimes stealing, sometimes working at menial jobs, and the abuse that naturally comes from life on the streets, had made a hostile, self-sufficient woman out of a girl that had lived but sixteen winters.

"Come, eat," said the old man. "Won't you tell me your name? Sharing names is like sharing bread. Many years have passed since I came to Tolden and still I find few who wish to share. It is a sad city--so unlike the days of my father's grandfather," he mused softly.

"If you must know, my name is Brinid," she said as she sat down on the low stool. "I don't give my name often, Old Man, so keep it to yourself. This is not just a sad city--it's horrible! What's there here for anyone except the King and his nobles? And please don't talk to me of the old days. Those are fantasy tales, and anyway, the past is best left in the past. Nothing good comes from remembering things that are long gone." Looking again at Lornen's face Brinid snipped, "And what cause have you to sit there so calmly?"

Knowing that she did not expect or even want answers to her questions, Lornen remained silent. Sadly he realized her need to masquerade as a boy. Listening quietly to an emotional tirade was usually best. He knew this from experience and thought it might defuse some of Brinid's anger. And gaining the confidence of this one so toughened yet so wounded would not be easy. Another day perhaps answers would be appreciated, if only she would stay long enough to hear them. It was obvious from the way she protected herself that she might never have known love or trust.

He wouldn't expect her to react with open arms to his gestures of kindness. The lessons his people had passed down from the lost Books made it clear that love is something that only flows freely between one who knows it and one who learns it. Encountering one who might have never experienced love called for patience and thick skin--for those times when the love would be thrown back at the giver with great force. Only after allowing enough time to pass for the unloved to catch a glimmer of hope would real love be possible--and even then it would be sorely tested and retested as the loved one began that path towards becoming someone who could freely receive and give love to another.

Lornen's thoughts were interrupted as Brinid's grouch started up again. He tried to listen intently as he chewed his piece of dark bread. "In this city all care only for themselves. We have to. How else could we fill our needs? Why do you share your meager loaf? If you expect anything from me, well, I have nothing to exchange." Lornen continued to chew softly and watch. His piercing eyes glimpsed a different girl underneath the dirt and hostility. The one he saw could become lovely and calm, but just now she was angry, covering over many years of hurt and disappointment. Perhaps she would remain long enough to hear reasons for his hope.

"I want no exchange, Brinid. What I have is not much, but it is yours. You may stay as long as you wish."

His sincerity coupled with the first bread she had tasted in days was confusing Brinid. Not wanting to be caught showing emotion, she looked down at her plate. Her usual street-wise defenses retreated slightly. Tired but a little relieved she thought, *I will keep a watch on this old one while I rest and regroup. He won't be strong enough to hurt me, anyway.* Had Lornen been able to see them, Brinid's eyes would have betrayed her uncertainty as she weighed the risks of staying here. Trusting no one was normal and comfortable, but the struggle to survive had taken its toll. "Thanks, Old Man," she said as she choked back tears and angrily finished her meal. Brinid rose from the stool, and almost like a cornered animal, backed her way into a far corner. There she sat down and wrapped herself in her cloak to wait out the night.

# # # #

Sometime after the mid hour of the night, Brinid stirred to a sound in the room off to her right. The old one was whispering with a figure in the doorway. Stifling her first impulse to jump up and flee, Brinid pretended to be asleep. Was the old man turning her in? She listened for a minute but could just barely make out a few words—"time," "battle," "wounded." It was not enough to really understand what was being said. *Oh well, he seems to have forgotten that I'm here and if it doesn't concern me I don't care.* She settled back down. *That old one surely is strange,* she whispered to herself as she drifted back to sleep.

Brinid next stirred with the morning light. For her first waking moments, she again pretended to be asleep and carefully observed the old man through barely open eyes. Her natural curiosity concerning who he was and what his midnight visitor had wanted were dampened by deeply ingrained habits of solitude and caution. Experience had taught her to keep things to herself and allow others to do the same--unless it would somehow give her an advantage. To stay successfully alive on the streets of Tolden required mainly two skills--cunning and dishonesty. This Lornen person seemed to possess neither. Clearly puzzled by this unusual old man, Brinid chose to remain quiet and watchful. She was almost certain that like everyone else, he too would eventually turn on her. *Never trust anyone--regardless of how good they might seem.* That was her tried and true philosophy. *Avoid hurt by relying on no one.* That was the only way to survive. Carried away by her musings, Brinid was startled when Lornen suddenly chirped, "Good morning, Brinid. Awaken to a new day. Come. Eat some porridge. I have an errand to do. Would you want to go with me?"

Brinid weighed her choices. *What have I got to lose,* she thought, *but a few hours? I'm sure the search for one more street thief was abandoned when they couldn't find me yesterday, and besides,* she thought, *maybe I can get another meal or two out of this old one.* Hunger overrode her well-ingrained habit of self-sufficiency and Brinid found herself agreeing to go. After eating the simple breakfast Lornen had offered her, she quickly gathered her simple belongings for their morning errands. She never let her meager possessions out of her sight, especially the precious knapsack that hung from her arm.

"All right, Old Man. I'll stick with you a while longer. I don't have any other business today." Brinid pulled her cloak around her shoulders and followed Lornen out the door.

A crisp quiet morning met them as most of the townspeople were just beginning to stir. Lornen walked quietly through the streets, as he pushed along a three-wheeled cart. Winding his way around the streets he seemed to have no apparent destination. The cart, covered with a tarp, looked like the ones that most Tolden vendors used to sell their wares. As Lornen effortlessly merged into the awakening market place, he became indistinguishable from any other vendor or shopper.

Brinid wondered just where he was going. Then an even bigger question began to form in her mind. *Why am I following him?* Surely no good could come of getting involved with another, she well knew from experience. Fresh in her memory, as if it were yesterday, was the time she spent with-- *NO! I will not think of those days! Keep your eyes on the old man,* she ordered herself.

Lornen continued walking through the city. Ever so often he would stop and talk to one or two other vendors. During these conversations, using no wasted motions, each vendor would put something into Lornen's cart. No one seemed to notice except Brinid. Curiosity was getting the best of her, but she knew better than to ask too many questions. She did not want any aimed back at her. After what seemed to Brinid like an hour of stop and go chatting, she followed along behind Lornen as he headed toward the outskirts of Tolden.

Having kept herself at a safe distance during Lornen's chats in the marketplace, Brinid now ran to catch up with Lornen and the cart. She was surprised to see strange bulges under the tarp. The wares the shopkeepers kept putting into the cart didn't seem to be enough to amount to this. Naturally suspicious, she wondered, *What ever is this old man up to?* Could it be something dangerous or crazy?

"I'm tired of walking, Old Man," she said aloud. "Where are we headed?"

"Wait here, Young One." I have to go a little further into the forest. I will return quickly."

Knowing the best way to stay out of another's trouble was by staying out of it, Brinid answered, "I don't care what you do, just get it done. I want to get back to the city."

Loren quickly disappeared into the trees, leaving Brinid propped in the shade of a huge rock. As she took a sip from her water pouch, she wondered, w*hy am I waiting here? I certainly know my way back,* but before she could finish thinking it all through Lornen reappeared, pushing a now empty cart. Their return to the small room where she had sought temporary refuge just yesterday was as uneventful and quiet as the morning had been puzzling to her. She decided to stop trying to understand what had been going on this morning. She had more than enough problems of her own without concerning herself with Lornen's strange activities. She reminded herself, *He's just a way to get the next meal or two.*

CHAPTER FIVE

Eric, Second Prince of Tolden, was not certain he would ever learn to use his Tazor as well as a Unidan could. The Tazor was a unique weapon that looked like a fancy sword. But the similarity ended there as the Tazor could also shoot forth a stinging burst of energy. Skilled users knew both forms of fighting. Eric already knew he was not cut out to be a fighter, and constantly hearing the rumors of the Unidans' expertise did not serve to boost his confidence any. To the contrary, he wondered if he would be able to fulfill the duties required of a Prince of Tolden. Although he did not always believe the tales he'd been told about Unidan skill, trainers continually insisted on using them as the standard. No one knew exactly why Unidans were thought to be the best, but he had heard whispers among the Tolden commoners that Unidan skill came from knowing something that Toldens did not know.

How annoying those Unidans can be, he thought, as he once again went through the drills with his Tazor. Some of the bursts of light found their place in the center of the target, leaving a smudge of black ashes at the middle of the hide. Tazors were one of the few remaining reminders of the power that had been possessed by the old ones of Atron.

The people of Tolden had long ago forgotten how the energy bursts actually worked, knowing only that that part of the Tazor was somehow powered by the sun. Rumor had it that the Ancients did not believe in killing, thus the secret for using Tazors to kill had been lost to everyone-- except to the Unidans--who were supposed to still possess this secret. Only by knowing this secret, or by fighting at a very close range, could a Tazor be fatal. This was why the Toldens did not rely much on the few Tazors they possessed. Bows and arrows and spears would find their mark and kill from a distance, and the Tazor was more likely to kill when wielded as a sword.

Eric treated the rumors about Tazors as he did many other rumors whispered about the city. It seemed quite unlikely that, from within himself, he or anyone else would be able to control the light of the weapon. Even his trainers could not do it, though they encouraged trying. Eric practiced often and diligently, but never seemed able to control the light other than manually, by pressing the red buttons on the handle.

Besides, he thought as he continued his routine of parrying, thrusting and then aiming to fire, *I have enough to think about by constantly having to live up to Stephad, First Prince of Tolden.* That title caused a great rivalry between the brothers, with Eric always the loser. Just because his birth preceded Eric's by twenty-three minutes, Stephad had always seen himself as the better--at least Stephad felt compelled to remind Eric of that every chance he had. Though they looked somewhat alike, both being strong and tall with soot brown eyes and very dark hair, the likenesses disappeared when one knew them better. It was easy to see in their eyes--Stephad's were piercing and hard while Eric's were kind and open. Stephad was intent on becoming a strong and commanding king while Eric loved to think about things of the heart, though he seldom felt free to let that be known. Nevertheless, Eric must be prepared to defend the city and their father's crown against the Unidans, whether they or his own people initiated the Raid. That was what was expected of a Prince of Tolden.

The scarceness of food from the famine is causing hatred of the Unidans to reach a boiling point here in the city, Eric reminded himself as he blasted a few more shots at the stained hide. Not only were their runners smuggling more grain out, Unidan slaves who worked in the fields seemed to escape much easier lately. The Unidan runners helped them without even bringing a raid upon the fields. Unidan workers were adept at keeping secret those who were helping them. *Well, there shall be less free Unidans and plenty more workers after tomorrow,* thought Eric. *Then we'll have plenty of slaves to build needed irrigation ditches from the river.*

Eric finished his practice and sheathed his Tazor. He would be ready when the call came to assemble at dark. In the morning they would raid the Unidan camp and take as many as they could surprise, killing as many as had weapons. Constant rumors in the city contributed greatly to the unrest among his people. The Unidans claimed that there was a way to save Atron and bring peace between the two peoples. Eric's father, King Krall, hated the Unidans for spreading their lore and causing his people to wonder and be stirred to unrest. No one could figure out exactly how the rumors had begun--rumors of a better way--but like the run-off from a bucket spilled in the streets, these rumors spread, seeping as it were under the cracks of every door in the city. Tomorrow's Raid would accomplish several purposes. First they would bring back extra workers for the fields and second, they would wipe out the source of all the rumors once and for all--the Unidans camp.

This was to be Eric's first raid and he already knew it would be difficult. Training and waiting had been all he could do thus far to keep the Unidans in their place. He was unsure how he would react actually fighting so close to the enemy. Deep down he had no desire to kill. He couldn't let anyone know his fears, certainly not his father or Stephad. Stephad surely would have no problem being ready tomorrow. His strong hatred of the Unidans was well known and his love of violence much admired. *I'll do my best to try not to think too much about what's happening tomorrow. I'm not ready to die,* he admitted to himself. Walking back to his rooms, Eric decided not to think about tomorrow's events any more today.

CHAPTER SIX

Candra was worried. She lay resting in her tent and thinking how the three months had passed so quickly since her Becoming Day. Her Father and Mother's tent had been extra busy since the day Candra brought the last message tube. Other runners had traveled each day, bringing grain as well as other tubes. Candra herself had only been out a few other times. That was not to the city, but only through the forest. Father had never allowed her to go to the city. She could meet other runners but never could she go past The Edge. Just this morning she knew there had been another Council meeting. How she wished she could have been there for the discussions and decisions that were made.

Nathan came bursting through the tent's door cover interrupting her thoughts, "Candra! Candra! Guess what? The people are preparing for a Raid. The Council is convening in the open place for immediate consultation with The One. Hurry! Now that you're a Participant we'll be allowed to go. Get your Tazor!"

Jumping to her feet, Candra grabbed her brother by the hands. "A Raid? Oh, Nathan, it has been so long since the last Raid, over seven summers. What did Father say? I knew something was going to happen."

Nathan answered, "He says that The One is leading us to be ready to defend ourselves. The latest message from our runners brought news that the Toldens are preparing to penetrate past The Edge and come right to our camp. Lornen sent word yesterday. Hurry, Candra! You can listen to the rest outside."

Even though Candra had been preparing for this moment most of her life, she could feel the fear rising inside, bringing questions to her mind. *Will our defenses be adequate? Who will die? Are Nathan and I really ready?* As she had been taught to do when fear rose up its head, she reminded herself of The One's truth: *throughout the years since the split between Unidan and Tolden, we Unidans have greatly desired for our world to be reunited. Now with the long drought, coming together is even more important. I have been preparing all my life for a day such as this.* With her fears a little calmed, Candra turned and quickly gathered her Tazor and cloak. As she left her tent and ran toward the Meeting Square, Candra thought back to Gran's words about fear and rehearsed them softly to herself: *What I feel is normal. It is not wrong to feel this way. The One is within and He takes care of me. Through Him I can face what I must--* "The Toldens are preparing for an attack," she heard an Elder say as she approached the Square. "Our runners have brought back word from the city that King Krall is angrier than ever. He is finished with us spreading our ideas and he has spent much of his energy convincing the Toldens that we are all crazy. The last time some of our people escaped from the fields he grew very angry. He cannot bear that we are successfully retaking our people. This time, the runners say, he plans to end the problems by going to the source. He wants to destroy our camp completely and keep only enough of us to work the fields."

Another Elder interjected, "Krall does not believe that we have power from The One and he does not want Toldens to hear anything about such power. He is planning to do as much damage to us as possible to keep his people from hearing truth."

Finally Handen spoke up and finished the meeting, "Some of you young ones do not remember what a Raid is like. It is horrible. People die and are wounded. I hope this one will be short and that it will not happen again soon. Now, here are our plans. The Council has communed with The One and each other. We are to go out and meet the raiders. This offensive move will surprise them and keep them from our camp. We need all Participants who are willing, to go while the rest stay here in the camp as backup."

Candra felt proud as she watched her father speak. He spoke with such confidence. His trust in The One was evident. Courage and faith shone on his face as he looked around into the faces of his family and friends. They had been through so much together. His boldness spread to each Participant as the Spirit of The One flowed over and throughout the camp. *This cause is worth dying for,* Candra thought as she looked around at her people. *We have to keep trying to reach the Toldens and find the lost Dome. Only through the One can the people get along with one another.* Gran had told her the Dome held the lost history of the Ancients and the written teachings of The One. Finding them would help the Toldens believe. Through believing The One, everyone would be able to learn to get along. But Candra had heard it said many times how hard it was to convince a Tolden that any of this was true. Abruptly the cheer rising from the camp brought her back to the present. Just hearing her people shout their confidence in The One lifted her spirits. As the meeting broke, the Participants began making preparations for what awaited them in the early morning.

# # # #

Before dawn the band of defenders from Unidan stole quietly out into the woods to set up their surprise defense. There were thirty men and women

Participants with Chregg, Borg, Marland and Richen the most experienced fighters. Handen had instructed them to lead the rest of the party. Chregg instructed the men and women to station themselves around the forest in pairs, forming a half-circle near the part of the Edge where the runner had indicated that the Toldens would enter to move towards the Unidan camp. They would have to cross the small clearing that lay just in front of the circle of Unidans. The archers climbed trees and hid in the dense branches, while the pairs with Tazors interspersed themselves among those who only carried Sedats.

Candra and Nathan were lying behind a large tree surrounded by underbrush, their Tazors ready. They could see the entrance to the Edge where the Toldens would approach. As Atron's sun broke the horizon Joden passed around the perimeter of hiding Unidans and whispered the blessing, "May the One have His way." She returned to Chregg and reported that all were prepared.

Nathan saw the first Tolden slinking carefully through the trees, dressed for battle in his leather breast cover, carrying his shield and spear. Quickly the others spotted more Tolden soldiers, a few with Tazors or spears and many with bows and arrows slung over their shoulders. At Chregg's command, the Unidan archers began loosing arrows upon the first unsuspecting Toldens that neared The Edge. After the initial pounding, the archers quickly climbed from their perches and joined the other Participants who, with Tazors set to stun, were running out of their hiding places, blasting at the soldiers. Tolden spears dropped to the ground before they could be thrown. More Toldens appeared from the trees, rushing closer to their targets in order to engage them with swords, leaving no room for archers to aim their arrows. Nathan and Candra now found themselves in the middle of a battle where they were surrounded by what seemed to be about fifty Tolden soldiers who were engaging most of the Unidan force in the clearing.

Well-trained in warfare, Nathan and Candra stood back to back, using their Tazors both as swords and as blasts of energy. They carefully aimed their Tazors to stun and not kill if it could be avoided. Though they had faced a heavy initial wave of arrows and Tazor blasts, the Toldens continued to fight with great ferocity. Anger from the surprise attack fueled their fury. A Tolden soldier came straight at Nathan, Tazor raised to strike. Together Candra and Nathan blasted him in the chest, using their power from the One. The energy pierced the leather breast cover, toppling the soldier in his tracks. Another came at Candra from the opposite direction. She engaged him sword to Tazor, parrying and thrusting while Nathan guarded her back. The Tolden moved towards her, and Candra knew she must set her Tazor to full power, but moments before she could send the fatal blast, Joden had stepped between them and struck the Tolden on his arm with her Sedat, knocking the sword from his hand. The Tolden soldier jumped to his feet, turned, and ran for The Edge. Candra sent a quick nod of gratitude to her best friend.

As the battle raged around them, Tazor energy lit the air as the Unidans used their power from The One. Swords clashed, but it was obvious that the Unidans were pushing the intruders back towards The Edge. Nathan focused on protecting himself and Candra. Sweat ran down his face and the smell of blood and burnt leather filled his nostrils. He just wanted it to be over. Speaking to The One aloud so Candra could hear, Nathan said, "Oh, True One, bring this battle to a quick close so that many can be spared." As Nathan finished speaking he saw a flash beside Candra as one of the Unidans blasted a Tolden that was aiming his Tazor at Candra's head from across the clearing. Nathan thanked The One and turned to engage the next soldier that came at them. Very slowly, the tide of Toldens inched backwards towards the way they had come. Some began to realize that perhaps the rumors in the city were true: these people did have some kind of extra power. Groups of soldiers began to turn and run, picking up wounded friends as they left. Their dead comrades were left behind.

Finally all the living Toldens were gone and the fighting stopped. Candra was exhausted. She and Nathan had proven their pledge of the months past as they fought back-to-back and side-by-side, watching and protecting each other. The surprise attack had been one advantage that drove the Toldens back past The Edge. But Candra acknowledged to herself that it had been the Power of The One in each Participant more than the use of the Tazor and good battle plans that served as the Unidans' true weapon. Years of training paralleled years of learning the teachings of The One. When each Unidan child received the One for himself or herself, His power came to dwell within the child. The child was never the same afterwards--how could he be with The One of the Ancients becoming his very life within.

Candra was thanking The One that the battle was over, at least for a time. She was not looking forward to experiencing this again soon. It was difficult to look around and see the people from both sides lying still on the ground. *Why, oh why could the Toldens not listen and believe? How much easier it would be for everyone,* her heart cried. As her eyes meticulously spanned the area, Candra spotted a sudden movement low on the ground, beside a fallen log. By the colors she could make out, she knew it was a Tolden. Cautiously she made her way towards the log, with her Tazor drawn. As she reached the man, Candra turned him over with her foot and aimed her Tazor at his throat.

Candra took a closer look at the man she held locked at the point of her Tazor. He was young, about her age. Blood was dripping from a cut on his head. His eyes closed, his breathing shallow, he seemed to be unconscious. *Gran will have to help him*, she thought. *His people ran off without him, thinking him dead. That's just like them. Look out for oneself--that was how they lived and fought.* As Candra looked around at the other Unidans who were checking through the woods, it appeared that no other Toldens survived. *We will bury their dead and take ours to the camp*, thought Candra. "Nathan," she called," get Chregg, please. A Tolden survived and lies here. He's wounded and unconscious. Gran can help him."

"Are you certain you have him under control?" asked Nathan.

"Sure, Nate, he's unconscious. We'll have to have some help to get him back to camp." As Candra continued to search his face for signs of awakening, her face betrayed the puzzlement she felt on encountering a Tolden up close outside of a battle. She'd been told many things about Toldens, but this one did not appear as different as she thought. There were no physical signs that he was any different than the Unidans.

The King exploded with rage, "You what! You did what! You've left Prince Eric behind? Imbeciles! Cowards! You will not live to see the morrow if you do not bring him to me immediately."

The company's captain stepped forward, "But, Sire, the Unidans caught us by surprise and fought so fiercely that we had no choice but to retreat. Those who could make it barely managed to escape. Eric fell with a wound on his head that had to be a fatal blow, and we only had time to see to the wounded."

"Enough. I do not want to hear excuses. Now out of my sight! Find my son or bring his body--whichever--I do not care. We cannot leave a Tolden prince in their hands. Report what you find to me in the morning or you will surely share his fate."

Stephad, First Prince of Tolden stood at his father's side. Stephad knew that his father's orders were more out of concern for propriety than for Eric himself. Stephad had been taught well by his father's example what to do in such situations. He would make a grand king when his father passed on--a mightier and stricter king than his father. He would end the raids and the Unidan rebellions once and for all. He admired everything his father taught him and knew it well. *Father grows older*, Stephad thought, *and I won't have much longer to wait. If Eric is truly gone, I have an open way to power. Eric, the inferior, will hardly be a threat, but just to be certain I will see to it that he is not found alive.* Stephad quickly left his father's presence to give special orders to his most trusted guard.

Nearing The Edge, the captain led his men cautiously through the trees. He crouched behind a huge rock and motioned the others to join him. "There may be Unidans on look-out," he said. "Let's wait until dusk before going in. Then we'll have just enough light to search the field where we left the prince." The four men in the company settled to wait. Their mission was doubly dangerous. The threat of Krall's rage should they fail clung to them like thick fog. They must find the prince or face the consequences of returning home empty handed.

At dusk, the captain whispered harshly, "Let's go. It should not take long to search the clearing where we last met these scum." Carefully they crept through the forest, entering The Edge. Though it was not guarded at all times, no one knew when that time might be. Unidans used their Tazors well and encountering them without several men in a band was dangerous. Approaching the clearing, all eyes began searching for evidence of Prince Eric's demise. Suddenly the captain spotted Eric's helmet, unmistakable because of the Tolden Royal Crest on its side. Nothing else was found. From all appearances, it seemed that Eric had died and been buried with the others who had been left behind. This would not be easy to tell the King, but at least they could give a report. The captain considered the response they would get. Prince Stephad supported his loyal guards and would stand for him and his men. The King, partial to the First Prince, might if the mood were right give only lashes for reporting without the prince's body.

Thunk! A Unidan arrow pierced the arm of one of the men standing beside the captain. If the Unidan archer had wanted, it could have pierced his eye. "Leave now!" a commanding voice boomed from behind a nearby group of trees. "Get out or the next three arrows will not be so nicely placed." The company, not wishing to fight with shadows, hurriedly turned and headed towards the city. Though they hurried to leave the Edge, they were in no hurry to face their irate king.

Overhearing the report from the search party, Stephad was greatly pleased to hear that no trace of Eric had been found. "Good," he snarled to the air, "that annoyance is gone for a while at least, perhaps even forever." His response betrayed his great dislike for his brother. His thoughts echoed the contempt. *I, Stephad am the First prince of Tolden. What use was Eric anyway? There's no need for a Second Prince. I, the First, will serve very well as King when Father is gone. And that day cannot come soon enough. Father has never done enough to pursue the ruin of Unidan, but I will take care of that when I am king.* Stephad's evil thoughts showed on his face as a deep scowl. *Unidans need to be totally subdued as slaves of Tolden—or else totally wiped out.* Stephad stomped from the court and headed for his rooms as his anger continued to boil. *Their talk of the old days is nothing but lies and stupid ideas. I do not believe one word. I will find a way to tighten the punishment for such talk from the captured Unidans. Keeping my own people in line is difficult enough without Unidans spreading their lies.* Stephad reached his room and ordered his evening meal. Removing his vest and slipping a robe over his shoulders, Stephad's thoughts continued. *The people may struggle with their crops and stores but a king's duty is to provide first for HIS needs and comforts.* In his heart, Stephad saw Unidans and Toldens alike as just here to serve the king. *When I am king,* Stephad finished his thoughts, *they will serve even better.*

CHAPTER SEVEN

Gran stirred the embers of her fire, raising a little flame that she blew upon softly while adding some kindling branches. She knew the others would soon return from the Raid and she would be much needed for her expertise with herbs and remedies. Close by Esleda and some of the other women were preparing food and bandages. From experience they knew that Tazor burns and cuts would not be the only wounds that needed attention. *How nice it would be to have the lost Books with their knowledge of cures,* Gran's thoughts drifted as she fed the fire. The books contained so many wonderful things from the past. The dire circumstances created by the famine made finding the books even more crucial.

Gran knew that the day might soon arrive that someone would have to venture out into the Beyond to look for the Dome, no matter the danger. Gran tried not to get discouraged over all the years that the parchment had been split. She maintained hope that perhaps The One would bring it to light before she went to be with Him. Her thoughts were interrupted by the sounds of the returning Participants. The women busied themselves with helping the injured Participants as Gran guided the worst of the injured to the pallets in her tent. Thanks to The One and the surprise of their defenses, few were badly wounded.

"Help them to pallets in here, Handen." Gran looked over at Candra who was there beside her father and spoke quietly to her, "Can you stay and help me? I know you're tired, but you may wash here if you're able to wait to rest." As Handen and his men carefully laid the wounded around on the pallets in Gran's tent, Candra hurried to wash and bring supplies over to the first person Gran was attending. As her grandmother worked, Candra began to speak softly about the battle.

"Oh, Gran, it was awful. I had heard the others talk of past Raids, but it was not as I imagined it would be. Everything happened so quickly and was so hard. Nathan and I fought beside each other just as we pledged. For so long I looked forward to being able to go out on a Raid, but now I hope it is a long time before I have to do this again. And did you see? One of these is a Tolden," she turned and pointed towards an unconscious man lying on a pallet across the room.

"I feel the horror of it with you, Beloved. Battles are never pretty or easy, even the ones we fight inside with the Tempter," Gran replied quietly as she walked towards the man that Candra had pointed to. As others bent to help the other wounded men and women, Gran bent to wash the gash on the young man's head, gently rinsing away the blood. She then carefully wrapped a soft bandage soaked with her healing remedies around his forehead, pulling the wound together. He did not awaken as she worked. The two women moved on to help bandage others after settling the Tolden. Soon each one of the wounded had been cleaned, bandaged, and comforted by someone from his or her family. They would rest here until they could safely return to their own tents.

When all the work was done, Gran called her beloved granddaughter, "Come here, Daughter of my son, she said patting the remaining pillows where she rested. "It is a sign of your dependence on The One that you can participate in the battle and then return to help with the wounded. Now it is your turn for healing, though your wounds are not visible to the eye."

Candra settled herself in her Gran's arms, resting her head upon her grandmother's beating heart. It did not take long for the tears to come. Though trained from childhood to defend her people, doing so was a shocking assault, not only physically, but to all she thought and felt. "Gran," she sobbed, "it was really terrible. I could not think too much about what was happening to us or to them. There were times that we knew the Tazor blasts were very strong. I so wish that the Toldens would listen."

Gran smoothed her brave Participant's hair and listened, understanding Candra's needs. She too had been a part of the Raids. She thought of her precious daughter, Jaslen, lost in a raid shortly before Handen and Esleda married. The pain of losing Jaslen never left, though it had dulled somewhat with the years. Only The One made it possible for her to bear it and hold no bitterness, as He had been her comfort all through these years.

Gran held and soothed Candra until the painful sobs diminished. Finally Candra said, "It is so wonderful to have your comfort, Gran. I don't believe I could bear this alone. Isn't it kind of The One to give us each other?"

"That is one of the best things about Him, Love-- that we are never left totally alone. Having each other, we see what He is like through each others' eyes, hands, words and comfort."

"Gran, some of my tears are for the Toldens who do not understand our ways."

Gran began speaking to The One. "Dear One, I thank you for my granddaughter's tears of cleansing and healing. As only You can do, take the shock and hurt into Yourself that she might go on as you wish. I don't ask that you take away her memories of this day, but that you give her a deeper knowing of Your care for our world. Strengthen her continued commitment to follow Your will in the repairing of our world."

"Thank you, Gran. I know Father and Mother are helping Nathan as well. He fought so bravely and kept me from getting wounded or killed." Candra managed a faint smile, "May I sleep here and help you through the night?"

"You may stay, Love, but there are others to help me while you rest. Battles take more out of us than we sometimes know.'

Candra snuggled into the pillows, dirty clothes and all, as Gran covered her with a shawl. "Thank you, O One. Bring us all back together soon, all of Atron," Candra murmured as she fell asleep.

# # # #

Eric awakened to pain, light, and the delicious aroma of stew bubbling over the fire. As he slowly turned his head to get his bearings, nothing seemed familiar. *Where am I?* he thought. The throbbing pain in his head made it difficult to think clearly. Gingerly his fingers searched for the source of the pain, finally touching a soft bandage. All at once he remembered. He had been in a battle near The Edge. He had camped there with his father's men, awaited dawn for a surprise attack. *We advanced toward the Unidan camp where we were the ones who were surprised*, Eric remembered. *We had barely penetrated the woods 1000 steps, before the Unidans were all over us. They were ready for us; hidden in places only they would have known. Though it was a fierce battle it wasn't too long before the Unidans routed our entire army, sending the survivors running for their lives back to the city.* Eric remembered being shocked by a Unidan Tazor and then hitting his head as he fell.

As his eyes scanned the room they came to rest on an elderly woman stooping to tend a fire. She was dressed in a maroon robe that fell to her feet and he guessed her to be an elder by the color of her soft white hair neatly braided and pinned at her neck. Catching his gaze the old one warmly asked, "How are you feeling, Young Man? Are you hungry?" She was already spooning the broth into a wooden bowl as she spoke. "I believe you could manage some soup broth. You've been asleep since they brought you in."

Eric tried to lift his head. "Now, please, don't try to get up," she continued, stooping down as she reached his pallet.

"Where am I?" Eric tried to demand though his voice betrayed his weakness. "Where is my Tazor?" he continued as his fingers felt around there at his hips where his weapon usually hung.

"There's no need to be alarmed, My Son. You were wounded and needing attention so our men brought you here to our camp," Gran said soothingly as she lifted the spoon from the bowl. "You were the only survivor of your people that did not run away. We have already buried your dead comrades and I treated your wounds while you slept. You've been sleeping for two days, but you must continue to lie still and be quiet." Gran waited quietly for the pale young man to take in all she was saying.

"I'm in the Unidan camp!" Eric, surprised and still disoriented, exclaimed as loudly as he could manage. He placed his hand against the throbbing wound on his head, "Why do you bother healing me when you're only going to execute me later!"

Gran shook her head slowly and her tones were gentle as she heard his lack of understanding. "Killing is not our way. We wish that there were never a need for bloodshed at all. Our wish is for peace and reunion between our people and yours--as there used to be long years ago. Our people went to The Edge yesterday only to defend our camp from the coming attack." Lifting the spoon again to the young man's lips, she entreated him, "Now here, you really need to eat."

As he watched Gran's gentle way and kind countenance, Eric felt the tension flowing from his body. He was surprised at how patiently she waited for him to open his mouth to take the spoon. He felt so weak, hardly ready for a fight, and his fear and anger had drained what little strength he had left after trying to talk. Somewhat grudgingly he relaxed onto the cushions.

Drained as he was, the young Tolden's thoughts were slowly considering a plan of action. *I must not let her know who I am. She might think differently about me if she knows I'm the Second Prince of Tolden. I will rest here as she suggests until I regain my energy and then I will escape.* Carefully, Gran spooned some delicious broth into Eric's mouth. *Her eyes are so warm,* he thought, *and her face, though lined, still seems serene. I don't think I've ever seen an old one look so untroubled.* After a few bites his eyes closed and once again he slept. He did not feel the loving hand that straightened his covers and brushed a speck of soup broth from his face. With the boy settled into the cushions again, Gran was free to turn her attention to the fire. She stirred what was left of the soup and then looked to other chores she needed to do.

CHAPTER EIGHT

From a pile of soft pillows across the tent, Candra often glanced up from her sewing to study the enemy from a distance. She was trying to repair the rips in a tunic she had worn during the attack at the Edge. As she sewed, her thoughts turned toward the strange young man her grandmother was caring for. Though an enemy, this one held a fascination for her that was disturbing. She had not even seen his eyes open since he had been brought to Gran, though Gran had said the last time he awoke he seemed a little stronger. Lost in her thoughts Candra blushed as she was caught staring at the injured one when he opened his eyes and looked directly at her. For the first time she heard the young man's voice, "Who are you?"

"I am Candra, daughter of Handen, granddaughter of Wilden," she said as she recovered herself and rose to one knee. Pointing to Gran over by the fire, she added, "and this is my grandmother. We all call her 'Gran'." Still a little embarrassed, Candra stood up and moved toward the fire as she spoke. "Are you able to sip more broth?"

"Yes, thank you," the stranger answered. As Candra moved to collect a wooden bowl, a spoon and some hot broth, Eric followed her with his eyes. He stared directly at her as she returned with his meal, taking in her long chestnut braid and very bright blue eyes. His intense gaze increased Candra's discomfort, making her feel both fearful and excited to be so close to this enemy while he was awake. Candra slowly spooned the warm liquid into Eric's mouth. She sensed by the look of fire in his eyes that being helpless was a hard thing for him to endure. Some of the tales she had heard of the Toldens spoke of their cruelty and extreme selfishness. Somehow, though his steady gaze was certainly intense, he did not exactly fit what she had thought to be true of his people. Perhaps she needed to practice what she was learning from The One: "Be slow to decide about another person solely upon a first encounter--even though that other might be your enemy." Though she had heard much about the people in the city, something about this young man confused her. Maybe she didn't have enough information to form an opinion. *For now,* she thought, *I'll be content with feeding him. I can talk later with Gran to help me sort through these new feelings. And The One has always been faithful to show me inside which new thoughts to sharpen and which to throw away.*

# # # #

Gran was sewing alone when Eric awakened a few days later. After sleeping almost constantly, he was beginning to feel a little more like himself again. *Maybe I can sit up,* he thought. He stirred on his pallet, rousing Gran's attention. "Good morning, Son of Tolden. The day is new and beautiful. I can see in your face that you feel much better."

"Thank you, Old Mother. It has been your care that has done it, I am sure--and someone else, I believe. I saw other hands helping me. Did I dream that?"

"No. That was Candra, my granddaughter. She has been here every day. She will come again."

The memory of that other face almost made Eric forget his desire to escape. He certainly wanted another look at that face while he was more awake. *My strength is gone*, he grumbled to himself as he struggled to sit up. His hand instinctively went to his side where his Tazor usually rested. *How can I defend myself? I must have my Tazor, or find someone else's. There is no guard here, probably because they know I'm still weak. And what was it he could barely remember the Old One saying--that they hate fighting? That's a little reassuring. I'll wait and watch. If what the Old One said is true, getting out will most likely be a simple matter when the time is right.*

With Gran's help and much straining and twisting, Eric had finally been able to sit up. With pillows piled behind his back and supporting him all around, Eric felt that he might be able to sit there for a while. It felt good to be off his back, even though walking still seemed a far away dream. That was going to take much more time.

"Happy morning, Gran," greeted Candra as she stepped through the tent door. "Oh! I didn't see that you were awake," Candra said shyly after spotting the young man from the corner of her eye. "And sitting up! What progress! I am called Candra--Beloved One."

"Good day, Candra. I am Eric and I have no idea what it means. Your grandmother tells me you've been helping me. I seem to remember hearing your name, though my mind is a little foggy on all that has taken place here. I thank you for helping me."

"I come here every day to help Gran and learn from her as well," Candra explained as she walked toward where Gran was working at the fire pit. "She's the wisest person in our camp and knows more than anyone about the lost ways, the lost Books and He who gave them to us. I wish to learn all that I can from her. You've been in good hands." Candra gave Gran a quick kiss on the cheek as she arrived at the fire. It felt difficult to look at the Tolden straight on.

Even though a little disoriented from his injury, Eric's memory had served him well. Just as he remembered, she was a lovely girl—yet not like the ones he had seen at court. *And she comes here to learn? I can't picture any of the girls at court having such a great desire to learn,* Eric thought, his eyes following Candra as she bent down to kiss the old one. *What are these Books she speaks of? And what does she mean by 'lost ways?' This girl's strange words pull at me to think more about them, though I know my mind should be on how I shall escape.*

Candra, felt a little ashamed of herself. *Here I am, next leader of Unidan, and I can't even look this stranger in the face.* She finally corralled her feelings at seeing the Tolden both awake and bright. Maybe it was easier to be near him when he was sick. *He is watching me very carefully*, she thought as she moved about the tent. The look in his dark brown eyes was unfamiliar to Candra, hard to read. Something hooded their meaning from her own discerning eyes, keeping her from seeing what he really might be thinking. Candra sat down near Gran and joined her sewing. She kept an eye on the new pot of soup that was simmering over the fire. This way she would be able to listen and watch the Tolden without seeming so conspicuous.

So his name is Eric, she mused. *Definitely a Tolden name; not like our own—each name carefully chosen for its meaning. He is different, but not so much as I'd imagined a Tolden would be.* 'The Tolden city is different from our camp,' she could hear the voices of the Elders saying when everyone was allowed to hear their talk in the Council. 'It's dirty and crowded with people, most of them being enemies of one another. They are always fighting and killing. And there are many young ones have no home to go to and roam the streets. It's very difficult for the people who are sympathetic to our Cause and stay there to help us. We thank The One for their courage.' Candra could not imagine how awful it must be not having a fire to warm oneself by or a family to love.

For his part, Eric seemed to be having just as many mixed emotions as Candra. He lay back down on his pallet and closed his eyes, resting his body from the strain of sitting up for the first time. One moment he thought of getting a Tazor so he could escape then he would find himself thinking about this curious girl who wanted to learn. *She speaks kindly, both to me and to the old one*, he observed. He had noticed the Tazor strapped to Candra's waist. *Where have they put my Tazor? How long will it take before I'll have*

2006 Barbara Moon

enough strength to find one so I can get away? I wonder if it's here somewhere in this very tent? Gran interrupted his thoughts as she knelt beside his pallet.

"More broth is ready, My Son. Can you hold it for yourself this time?" asked Gran as she offered the bowl.

"I think so. Yes," answered Eric. He glanced at Candra, now remembering that she had not only spoken to him, but had fed him days before. He took the bowl and managed to spoon a little bit of it into his mouth. *It won't be many more days now until I'm ready to get away*, he thought as he ate, feeling stronger with each bite he swallowed. *I will think of something*.

After finishing the soup and setting the bowl beside his pallet, Eric slid his aching body down into the pillows and watched the two women sew until he once again drifted to sleep.

CHAPTER NINE

Awaking a few mornings later, Eric told Gran, "I believe that I'm ready to stay up today, Old One. Your care has returned my strength to me. I don't know how I can repay you for your care and kindness."

"Your return to health is all I seek, Young One," Gran smiled as she brought his meal. "I will tell the Council you are almost well. Then they will decide what is next for you."

Eric felt very uncertain about what he wanted the leaders' decision to be. He knew he did not yet want Gran or the others to know who he was. *Maybe I'm not so sure just who I am myself,* he mused. The last few days, when he'd had to remain resting on the cushions, there had been ample time for thinking. He often listened to Candra and Gran's conversations, as well as to those of others who came and went through the tent flaps. Each one spoke of things he did not understand. Their ways with him and with each other were very different from anything he could remember experiencing. Watching them interact with each other stirred a longing so deep in his heart he was almost afraid to acknowledge it. That longing was for his mother who had died when he was very young. He could hardly remember what she looked like.

There's something different about these Unidans, he noted to himself as he scraped the last bit of broth from the bowl and set it aside. *Whatever that difference is, it draws me.* Eric was beginning to admit to himself how lonely he had been at court. Stephad and their father were so alike, so close to each other, they'd often shut him out of plans and conversations. *I should be plotting my escape from this hated enemy camp, yet I lie here wishing I could stay forever.* His eyes closed, Eric listened as Gran chatted with yet another woman who had come into the tent to seek her counsel.

#

Later that week, Candra burst through the tent flap only to find Eric standing, talking quietly with Gran. Surprised by this newest development, she stopped. Quickly recovering her enthusiasm, Candra said, "Hello, Eric. How wonderful to see you're strong enough to get up and walk around. I'm glad you're up." Before she could catch herself, she turned to Gran and exclaimed with joy, "Gran! I have an idea. It's a beautiful day! Do you think your charge might be ready for a short walk? It would give me pleasure to show him our camp."

"Your Gran has already said I can be out, but someone has to be with me until the Council decides what to do about me," Eric answered with a grin. "I love your idea." Seeing the nod and smile from Gran who was not at all perturbed that she was unable to get a word in edgewise, the two disappeared through the tent flap.

Walking slowly to the thin stream behind Gran's tent, they sat on a large rock and stared peacefully at the trickling water, made so much smaller now with the long draught. The forest sounds around them blended with the sounds from the camp. To Eric it was like a paradise. He knew nothing like this in the city. The people there did not know much about peace. As if reading his thoughts, Candra said, "Eric, you should see the creek as it was before the drought. Water tumbled and gurgled through the camp, instead of just trickling as it does now. Our forest provided all we needed except for the grain for bread. Now we have little of either, as the animals in the forest are also suffering."

"It grows worse in the city, too" replied Eric. "Irrigating the fields becomes more and more difficult with each passing week. If only it would rain," he sighed, "so many months without rain."

"Gran says there is a way," said Candra quietly.

"And what is that?" asked Eric with surprise.

"It's rumored that your people don't believe there is a way," she answered. "I'm not certain if I should tell you."

"Maybe this Tolden is different, Candra. Please?" he urged. "Try me. If I start to laugh, you can stop."

Candra glanced up to see if Eric were mocking her. His face seemed sincere. "Maybe Gran should tell you. She knows the most about the things of Atron, more than anyone I know. She can tell you about things of the Past, the Books, The One."

Eric found himself eager to hear what the Old One had to say, though he could not explain why. A Prince of Tolden--listening to a Unidan old one? A Unidan would never be allowed in the court to talk so with anyone, much less a prince. That would be unheard of. "I heard you speaking another day of these books and The One. Every Tolden I know believes this talk is rubbish." Eric paused, deep in thought. "Yet you seem to change when you speak of these things," his eyes focused piercingly on Candra's face. "Your face, your voice, they change—as if you are somewhere else. What is it that changes you so? I'm curious. What does it all mean?"

"Are you sure you really want to know?"

Somewhat surprised at the intensity of his own longing, Eric found himself replying, "Yes! Yes I do."

Slowly Candra began to talk. "The One is the creator of all worlds and all peoples. We Unidans believe that He comes to live inside of all who ask Him to. When He comes to live inside you, things change. Somehow He changes us from bad to good, becoming entwined in our very own life, forgiving us all our wrongs from the past and even those that will happen in the future. We have been made good with His goodness, but can still choose to do right or wrong things. As we grow stronger in our belief that He is our very life, we're more we're able to see His ways and follow them. He teaches us from within how to truly love and live at peace with one another." Looking at her new friend, Candra asked again, "Are you certain you want to hear this?" At his nod of assent, she went on.

"Unidan families are close and caring. When we have disagreements, we discuss things instead of walking away or hurting someone. We don't harbor secret hurts and let them grow. The One Within makes each sensitive to the other so that we cannot remain apart very long with our hurts. He meets every need we have and that makes it easier to love one another. There is no need to hate, steal or kill. What belongs to one belongs to all because knowing The One helps us become like family. He is all to all. We can seek any kind of help from one another and the Council is here for everyone. The One's power is ours when we need it, as we give everything we are to Him and trust Him to lead us from within." Candra looked up again to read Eric's face. It was puzzled but not mocking.

"Our power is in our Tazors and our training, things we can see and touch," he stated. "We have no need for crutches such as you describe-- magical and invisible."

"He is not a crutch, Eric the Tolden," Candra protested gently. "He is a person."

"Well, go on, please, Candra the Beloved," Eric responded with a smile. "I do want to hear more. Tell me about the books?" It was much easier to listen to these rumored tales when he could hear it from her beautiful face, full of expression. In fact, he found himself liking to hear about the many things that were different about her people.

"The Books are from the Ancients, books from The One. We think that the Ancients lived even before the Two Kings of Atron, and of course The One has always been. The books tell the stories of the beginning of Atron, the story of The One and His ways. Since these books have been missing, we have lost much of the Ancients' knowledge. Gran believes their ways of healing were better than her herbs and she thinks what they knew would help us find a way to end this drought. But wait!" Candra interrupted herself. "I'm telling you too much. Gran and Father will decide what more you can know." Standing up from her rocky perch, Candra signaled an end to their discussion. Motioning for Eric to follow, she said, "Come. Let's return to the tent before you tire."

"If you insist, Teacher," Eric teased, as he looked straight into her beautiful, clear eyes. "I must admit your kindness to me and what you've said so far make me very interested in hearing more of your stories. Please tell Gran that I am serious about learning more of your ways. Will you?"

Though it was difficult, Candra kept her eyes locked with Eric's. New emotions stirring in her heart were very confusing. She felt herself blushing, and softly murmured, "I will tell her," as she turned to go.

# # # #

Later while Eric napped, Candra and Gran sat on a log outside the tent. They were enjoying the afternoon warmth, their morning chores finished. Candra began telling Gran about her conversation with Eric. "Gran, I don't know what all these feelings are about. This Tolden is not at all like I imagined one would be. He's closed up, yes, more than we are, but not cruel or ugly. Is this part of my learning?"

Gran reached out to touch Candra's hand as they sat listening to the chirping birds and other chattering animals. "Yes, My Beloved. You have heard the words of The One--to love as He loves--but here in Unidan it has been easy." Candra listened carefully as Gran continued. "Your feelings are confusing, perhaps, because you are feeling some new ones mixed in with the old. The deep love of The One is expressed in many different ways. Is this perhaps a tasting of the love between a man and a woman?"

Again Candra blushed, her feelings a jumble, as Gran went on in her wise way, "Is there some fear here that maybe the love is of this kind? Through you The One loves all. How you allow that love to come forth out of you is a combination of your choices and Him."

"I *am* afraid, Gran. He's a Tolden? I cannot let myself feel this way. He doesn't know The One." Candra laid her head on Gran's shoulder. "Why did he have to come here? I don't even want to think about it."

"The One has His plan, and the Tolden is part of it. The One will help. Remember, you know inside, My Beloved, what you are to do. Rest in The One. He will work out your steps, your needs. You don't have to know all things today."

"Eric says he want to know more of Atron and the Books. I am not certain of his reasons, so I left it for you. Will you talk with him?"

"Of course I will, dear Candra. You know talking of them is my favorite thing to do." Gran lifted Candra's chin and softly kissed her cheek. "Perhaps we will speak of several things, but we must not speak of the parchment or the Dome." Gran stood up to go and begin the evening meal as Candra turned toward her own tent, stopping first at Nathan's to hear about his last run to The Edge.

"Hi, Companion," quipped her cheerful brother as Candra pushed aside the tent flap after calling out his name. "How goes the Tolden visitor in our midst? Has he noticed how lovely you are?"

"As a matter of fact, Dear Brother," Candra returned smugly as she entered the opening, "I have just returned from a walk with him."

"Oooooooo!" her brother teased as he touched her hand, pulling her to sit beside him at his fire. "I must exercise my pledge as your First Companion today then."

"Seriously, Nate, I do need your help. My feelings are all over the place. A Tolden?" she queried, taking a seat on some pillows. "What am I thinking? What could The One use this for? Is it He? Am I crazy?"

"As your wise and serious Companion, my dear sister, I will admonish you to be cautious and slow," Nathan said, deepening his voice, and then adding with a smile. "But most of all, I wish you to be honest and true." "The One knows all things and sees the whole picture." Nathan's voice was changing back to its normal tone as he finished. "He will show you in His time. Say what is true to the Tolden and walk in patience."

"Patience," Candra said thoughtfully. "There it is again. Thank you, Most Wise One, for your words of truth. I know I can count on you to be watching." Candra stood and then left for her own tent, pondering the unusual events of these past few weeks.

CHAPTER TEN

Brinid and Lornen had been skirting the edge of Tolden's marketplace for almost an hour. Brinid could not figure out how one so old could keep such a pace. She had underestimated the old man's strength when they first met. At last Lornen seemed to sense it was a good time to move into the lines of other city dwellers who were hurriedly making their way to the West gate, then drifting towards their huts. Curious and bored as usual, Brinid continued to follow Lornen.

Security was tighter now since the last Raid. The king's guards eyed each person closely, seizing an occasional bag or poking their sticks into vendors' carts. The lack of rain was making everyone edgy. Lornen, so ordinary and harmless, slipped past the guards without inviting even a look from them. Once outside the gate, Lornen turned towards a path that would lead them past some of the fields and huts where the grain growers and the workers lived. Brinid shuddered as they passed the huts. She remembered what being taken there had been like and did not want to think about having to go there again.

"What are you doing, Old Man? I am tired of following you around in circles. I have better things to do with my time," grumbled the girl who had seldom left his side since meeting him.

Ignoring her complaints, Lornen turned from the cart path into the forest. This wasn't the first time Brinid had followed Lornen outside the city. Brinid hesitated, but did not want Lornen to see the fear burning her stomach. She had never gone into the forest with him and this was not the first time he had brought her near to it. She did not like even being close to it. Signaling her to come closer to his side, Lornen whispered, " You may return if you like, My Child, and wait at my door for me. I won't be much longer. The last part of this mission I must do alone anyway."

"What difference will it make if I wait? Here or there--door or tree?" snapped Brinid. "Waiting is part of the day. I choose to wait here. I can see the cart path from here without being seen if I wish it. What have I to lose? Go on!" Brinid's face did not show her fear. *No one shall know when I feel afraid,* she reminded herself. *Weakness is not to be tolerated.* She would wait alone at the fringe.

Today was Brinid's fifteenth day with Lornen. T*he longest I have been with anyone since my last stay in the grain field,* she thought. *Why do I continue to follow the old one around . . . especially to this part of the countryside?* Somewhere along the way she had quit thinking of Lornen as her next meal. *He is so different than anyone else I've been with. What is it?* That curiosity was chipping away at her reserve.

Torn between the strange fear of the forest and her desire to be with Lornen, Brinid decided to follow him. *I'd rather be near Lornen,* she thought. *How does he make his way without any visible markers?*

Just before she caught up with Lornen, Brinid saw someone step out from behind a tree and speak quickly with Lornen. The stranger was covered from head to toe with a brown woven cloak, his face hidden by the hood.

70   2006 Barbara Moon

Sensing she had seen something she shouldn't have, Brinid quickly made her way back to the fringe and sat down, pretending she had not seen Lornen with the stranger. She sat there lost in thought. *Lornen always returns to the city with his cart looking the same. Maybe tonight I will ask him what he was up to. It isn't so bad being with someone these last days,* she admitted to herself reluctantly. He was kinder to her than anyone she had ever known.

"Old Man!" exclaimed Brinid, "You startled me." Brinid was not accustomed to being caught off guard. Shaking her head to clear it, she quickly gathered her belongings and followed Lornen back to the cart path. Brinid frowned. *I want to know what is going on, who that other person is.* Well trained by years of solitude, Brinid could not seem to find the words to ask what she wanted to know. As she was gathering her courage to speak to Lornen, already near the edge of the cart path, two city guards approached Lornen, pointing their spears at him. Brinid quickly ducked behind a large bush and pulled her hood over her head. Never one to get too close to the king's guards when it could be avoided, she peered cautiously through the leaves.

"Come on, Old One. Just what is your business here? We want to ask you some questions."

"I have done nothing wrong," Lornen protested quietly as he bent over the cart to adjust the cover. One guard poked Lornen's ribs with his spear while the other guard began to search the cart by jabbing at its cover. Lornen jumped back, reaching for the Sedat beneath his cloak, distracting the guards as their heads spontaneously turned at the movement. Suddenly the cover flew off the cart as a young man sprang from it with his Tazor already drawn.

Brinid saw two simultaneous flashes and then both guards fell to the ground. "Hurry," said the stranger she had seen talking with Lornen as he began to drag one guard from the path. "They are only stunned."

Before Brinid could think of a reason not to help, she found herself darting from behind her bush and grabbing the stunned guard by his belt. Lornen glanced over at her with surprise, as they quickly finished moving the cart and the other guard to the woods. The young stranger barked sharply, "Hurry! Further into the woods! We have no time to lose. Other city guards may be awaiting their return."

Seeing Brinid's hesitation at the command, the young man grabbed her arm. "Who are you?" he demanded.

"This one's with me," Lornen explained. "We'll have to take him with us. They'll hurt him if he's caught."

Brinid struggled but could not free her arm from the young man's grasp. "Let me go!" she yelled, only to have a hand, attached to a strong muscular arm encircle her head and clamp over her mouth. "Quiet! Do you want to bring more guards upon us?" the stranger hissed. "Come on!"

As the young man began dragging her towards the deeper shade of the forest, Brinid became frantic. *I cannot go in there!* Her eyes were wide with fright. Lornen had seen them ablaze with anger, but never with fear. He paused and laid his hand upon the young man's shoulder. Touching the hand covering Brinid's mouth, Lornen said, "Just a minute, Nathan. Let me talk to him."

"Alright, but make it quick!" And to Brinid, "You must stay quiet, Boy. Will you be quiet if I remove my hand?" The cloaked head underneath his hand nodded as the terrified eyes locked onto Lornen's as soon as the hand dropped. Brinid stood to her feet facing Lornen.

Lornen looked at Brinid with compassion. "We have to take you with us. You will not be safe back in the city because of what you've seen. The king has ways of convincing people to tell things they have seen. There is no going back. You will have to trust me. I know you haven't trusted anyone for a long time; maybe never. You can come willingly and quietly, or by force, but you have to come."

Brinid had never told anyone when she was afraid. *I don't even know why I am so afraid of the forest*, she thought. "It's the forest," she growled. "That's what I don't know about. Maybe you've been feeding me and so far you haven't tried to harm me, but I've never been in a place like this."

Lornen sensed more than heard a small change in Brinid's tone. Perhaps his steadfastness was helping her trust. "Facing your fears with someone you know will help you, and since I am the only one here you've met before, then I'll have to do. We *have* to go. Come. Walk between us. We know the forest. You'll be safe between us. You can walk in our knowing."

Brinid's eyes softened and for the first time Lornen saw her relax. She swallowed hard, set her chin and reached for his hand. "If I have to go with you, I will walk. I'll not be dragged or carried.

# # # #

After about twenty minutes the young man slowed his pace. There were no markers or signs. Brinid could not figure out how they knew which direction to take, but she had found her heart pounding less and less as they continued to walk. Nothing crossed their path that would alarm a city dweller and after a time, the cool shade of the forest seemed soothing instead of frightening. *I guess it was the unknown like Lornen said,* Brinid pondered. *I am seeing there is much unknown to me. Lornen is different--even taking time to explain to me when he could have left me there, or forced me.* Just then she heard a faint whistle and a soft swoosh of air between her shoulder and Lornen's. Stopping in mid stride, Lornen bent to pick up an arrow tipped with brown feathers that had flown perfectly between him and Brinid.

Seeming to talk to the air Lornen spoke aloud, "It is us, sentry--Lornen and Nathan. Things have not gone as planned and we must hurry to speak with Handen.

"Pass into the clearing so I can see you better," replied the sentry.

The three stepped forward and two sentries dressed in forest colored clothes with brush stuffed in their hats sprang from their hidden perches in the trees. "Who is this one?" one of them demanded. "You I know, and Nathan, but him I do not," he said pointing to Brinid.

"This one is with me. You will have to trust my judgment," answered Lornen.

"Alright, go on. Handen expects you. We sent one of our men in as soon as you said your name."

Brinid was more than a little confused. Her face almost hidden by her hooded cloak allowed Brinid to watch without the fear of being scrutinized herself. *Where are we?* she wondered as she looked around at the camp. Nearing the largest tent near the center of the camp, Brinid watched carefully as a beautiful young girl ran towards them and gathered the rough young stranger into a big hug. "Nathan, Nathan! What has happened? You were supposed to be going to Tolden as part of a rescue party to help free some of our people from the fields! You're back too soon. Are you all right?" Hardly stopping for breath she continued, "I told Father I should go instead of you. I was worried that something might happen!" Candra's voice trailed off as she noticed the stranger standing beside Lornen.

"Oh! Something serious must have happened to make you bring a stranger back to camp. Tell me, please."

"Calm down, calm down," Nathan said soothingly to his sister as he hugged her again. "We're alright. Do you so quickly forget power and protection of The One who is with me? Let us pass by and you can hear the whole story." Motioning toward Brinid Nathan explained, "This is a friend of Lornen's. We had no choice but to bring him with us as he saw too much and would not have been safe in the city. Come. Let's go talk with Father and the Council."

As the four entered the Council tent, Handed walked quickly to hug his son. Others greeted them as they found their places in the Council circle. Then Lornen and Nathan recounted the story of how they were ambushed by guards at the cart path. This helped explain why they had returned to camp so soon—and with a stranger. Talk soon turned to the subject of what to do with the two Toldens who were now in their midst, confirming Brinid's deepest fears.

I am with the Unidans, she realized. That possibility had been nagging at her since they entered the forest, yet nothing she was experiencing or seeing with her own eyes seemed to line up with her ideas of what Unidans were like. She had always hated them. *Unidans killed my parents, didn't they? These people have not even taken the time to bind my hands.* Her thoughts turned to Lornen. He had always treated her kindly, giving her bread or stew when she was hungry and patiently explaining things she did not understand. *And,* she mused, *he hasn't told them I am a girl.* Still greatly confused Brinid continued to keep her own counsel while she listened from within the darkness of her hooded cloak.

As the talk seemed to come to an end, all eyes turned towards Brinid. *Where is the other Tolden they speak of?* she thought, as Handen asked her to stand. "Well, Young Man, we will leave you in Lornen's continued care until further changes are necessary. Only Unidans can find their way in and out of here and the sentries are well aware of all comings and goings. May The One make Himself known to you while you are a guest in our midst." After dismissing the Council, Handen drew first his son and then his daughter into each of his arms and reminded them, "The other Tolden is free to leave Gran's tent as long as someone accompanies him. We will talk more about what we must do with these guests tomorrow. Come, Beloveds and enjoy some stew and conversation with your mother and me."

Brinid followed closely behind Lornen as they exited the Council tent. Still a little unsettled inside and feeling lost in the midst of these strange people, she matched her steps to Lornen's as he moved towards a smaller tent set near the trees a little further down the path. Between that tent and the next lay a small, well-tended garden, the plants sparse, but green in spite of the drought. As they approached the small tent, for the second time in her life Brinid could not find it in herself to react with her usual hostility. All that had happened was too strange and unexpected. "Old Man," said Brinid finding her tongue, "I do not wish to remain here. Take me back to the city. You have no right to keep me here with these people. I hate Unidans and want nothing to do with them."

"Brinid," said Lornen, bending to look under the hood of her cloak and straight into her eyes, "I am a Unidan. Do you also hate me?"

Brinid could not answer. Her chin dropped and she stared at the ground. Lornen touched her shoulder kindly and continued towards the tent. *This old one does not understand and he asks questions that are too difficult to answer,* she thought as she again followed Lornen's lead. *I will have to do as he says until I find this other Tolden they spoke of. Then we can plan our escape together. How could I possibly want to stay with Unidans?* Lornen opened the tent flap and ushered her inside. This was the tent that he always used while he was in camp. Once Brinid was safely inside, Lornen walked a little further to collect some wood for a fire. Brinid settled herself and her knapsack into one corner of the tent. Hugging her knapsack close to her body sometimes gave her comfort. It was all she had and she guarded it jealously, never allowing anyone else to touch it. As she rested in the bit of comfort there in the corner, Brinid realized how very tired she was. Much had happened this day, causing both turmoil and fatigue. *Was it only this afternoon that we hid the stunned guards and entered the woods?* That event had drastically changed her life. *No longer on my own and free,* she stewed.

I'm now a prisoner of the hated Unidans. Thinking of Unidans reminded her of her parents and that made her wonder for the thousandth time: *Who am I? Why am I so alone?* Somewhere in her faded memories she could see a face telling her that the Unidans were at fault. Being here in their camp felt very confusing.

# # # #

Candra and Nathan were finishing the evening meal in their parents' tent and discussing the day's events with Handen and Esleda. Conversation moved quickly from one subject to another: Two Toldens in their camp. Two guards stunned and hidden from pursuers. Plans to free more from the fields thwarted. Nathan and Lornen almost caught by Tolden guards. As always the talk turned to the need to find the Books and the Dome. There were so many things wrong on Atron and so many needs in both Unidan and Tolden. "We must keep looking to The One. He will show us," Candra said, as the others nodded in agreement. "I thank Him again that you returned safely, Brother."

"I am thankful, too," said Nathan humbly. "We're trained to react in defense, but it was still a close call. This hatred and killing will stop only when the people of Atron are reunited under the One." As the brother and sister rose to take leave of their parents, Nathan whispered to his sister. "Let's ask Gran and Father again about going out without the other parchment."

"Yes," Candra answered. "I've asked before, but now we're both of age and much stronger. Things keep getting worse and worse. Let's talk to Father, Mother and Gran in the morning."

# # # #

Two days had passed since Brinid found herself in the Unidan camp. She had not ventured out of Lornen's tent. She ate what he put in front of her, but with little enjoyment. She felt very restless, but did not want to encounter any other Unidans. Her hope was that she might be able to overhear something about the other Tolden that would help her escape, but the fear of being outside overrode that hope. The inner struggle brought feelings of hopelessness and anger. Sleep was her only break.

Brinid always slept holding her knapsack, never letting it out of her sight. Hidden inside were her eating utensils, a change of clothes and her most prized possession. It was really just a worthless piece of parchment, but it had been with her ever since she could remember. Somehow she knew that it was a slim link to her past--whatever it was--and she guarded it fiercely.

Although she seldom looked at it, she was ever aware of its presence and its presence always brought her a small bit of comfort. *Maybe now would be a good time,* she tried to sooth herself, *to just take out the parchment and look at it for a moment.* Carefully Brinid drew out the pouch that covered the parchment. Just touching it brought the comfort she needed as she gently pulled the parchment from its pouch and unfolded it. Brinid lightly touched the torn edge that indicated that the parchment had once been larger. The words and drawings made no sense to Brinid, but she loved to look at them and wonder what they could mean.

Lost in her despair and daydreaming, Brinid was unaware when Lornen bent to enter the tent, bringing her some stew. He quickly retreated for a moment and made some noise outside the tent. Brinid hurriedly stuffed the parchment back into her sack. All the mixed emotions were making her too tired to think anymore and she did not really want to eat. Cradling the knapsack in her arms, she curled her body around it and went to sleep.

CHAPTER ELEVEN

Brinid's stay as a "guest" of the Unidan camp had now stretched to a week. Now and then she ventured from the tent to get some fresh air, but she still mostly kept to herself in Lornen's tent, wondering if Lornen had seen her parchment and fearful that he might try to take it away from her. It was literally all she had to call her own.

Still, her self-imposed isolation was causing her thoughts and feelings to boil. Her fear of the woods seemed mild compared with the desperation she felt as each day brought more loathing about her sudden loss of freedom. Most days she sullenly refused to talk with Lornen and only left her corner when she wanted to eat. Lornen did not pressure her, only now and then encouraging her to come out and be with the others. Blinded by her fears and anger, Brinid simply could not see that her lack of freedom was of her own making.

As Brinid stewed one morning, it finally came to her. *I know how I can leave this place. No one knows that I have my Sedat in my boot. I can use it to get a Tazor.* Never mind that she had never held one. *I can figure that out,* she assured herself. She quietly left the tent with her belongings, keeping her head and face more covered than usual. Outside, in a section of the camp near the Meeting Square, Candra and Nathan were practicing with their Tazors. Brinid leaned against a tree to watch. Tazors were valuable, not only as weapons, but because there were not many left and they brought a good price in the city. *Everyone wants one,* she planned, *and I can name my price.*

Brinid was watching two very skilled users. Skill comes from balancing burst-strength with distance and Brinid was astonished at how accomplished both Nathan and Candra were with their Tazors. She could see that these two users both knew the secret of the Tazor. Like those who did not know the secret, they skillfully used the Tazor as a sword. But these two knew as well how to control the bursts of energy without changing the settings for the power. Because they did not have to use the buttons on the handle, they were extremely faster than anyone Brinid had ever observed. She did not know that the secret skill came from their knowledge of The One. His own power was available to them as they walked through life, and when using the Tazors, they trusted that power to control the bursts of energy. Too much too close would kill, too little too far away would allow the opponent to return his fire. Those who did not know The One were only able to use the Tazor as a sword with sporadic bursts of energy as they changed settings with the red buttons.

In Unidan, over-sized dummies stuffed with mud and grass, served as targets for practice. Deeply ingrained in each Unidan was the understanding that all this power was simply to be used to defend themselves in a Raid or a life-threatening situation.

All Unidan Participants were skillfully trained in the fine points of using of the Tazor and would stun rather than kill whenever possible. The trick to stunning was to hit the opponent in places that would cause him to drop his weapon, while at the same time keeping oneself a moving target. The intensity of the Tazor beam could also be lowered so as to cause only a shock where it touched. Only during the full battle of a Raid would they set to kill. Unidans could do these various settings of energy as quick as a thought, as they tapped into the power of The One in them.

From a near by log, Eric was also watching Candra and Nathan practice. As he watched in amazement, the skills he had only heard rumors about stirred his thoughts about life in the Unidan camp. The two opponents finished their practice and walked over towards Eric's log to rest, each sitting on either side of him. He had been told that no one could get out of the camp without a guide, *but shouldn't I be trying?* He questioned himself. *And what will I do when I return to Tolden? Tell my father how wrong everyone is about the Unidans? He won't listen even if I have proof.* As he weighed his observations back and forth in his mind, he realized that the last few days he had become totally uncertain of what he really wanted. *And what do I do about Candra? Leave and never see her again? Fight her some day in another Raid?*

Just as Eric was about to speak out loud, a blur of brown flashed by the corner of his eye and knocked Candra off of the log down onto the ground. It was that other boy who had come into camp with Nathan a week ago. Quickly Eric saw that the boy was going for Candra's Tazor while holding a Sedat in his hand.

Eric jumped to his feet, grabbed the other Tazor from Nathan's loosened grip, and turning the sword flat, he struck the boy on the hand. The boy yelped, dropping his Sedat and covering the injured hand with his other. Candra swiftly rolled to a seated position astride his chest, gaining a tight grip on both his hands, holding them tightly in hers. Nathan, at first seemingly paralyzed but now in motion, quickly joined her, separating the boy's hands and pulling them over his head, pinning them to the ground. Thrashing and struggling to get loose, the boy rolled part way over and back. The hood falling off of his head revealed two long braids of raven hair, which flew around a scowling, angry face with green eyes that seemed to be spitting fire.

"A girl?" Nathan exclaimed, almost forgetting to hold onto the flailing hands. "You're not a boy--you're a girl!" he stammered again.

"Aren't you the brilliant one," spat Brinid. "Let me go!" Candra moved off Brinid's chest, staring at the smudged face, but keeping her guard. Brinid sat up as Nathan moved back one pace, ready to pounce again if needed. The commotion brought others running, including Handen, Gran and Lornen.

"She's a girl, Gran," Nathan sputtered again.

"I can see that, Nathan," replied Gran bending down to look at the girl's hand. "Come, Daughter, let me see to your hand," soothed Gran, reaching out to Brinid as Handen bent to help Candra to her feet. Lornen also stooped beside Brinid and encouraged her to follow Gran into the tent. "I can go on my own, Old Man," she growled, though the fight and anger were slowly leaving her. She did not like being the center of attention, and the sooner inside, the better. Besides, the Tazor had hurt her hand.

As the three went into Gran's tent, Nathan and Candra noticed that Eric stood there with a Tazor in his hand. Eric looked down at his hand as if in a trance. He had acted so quickly; the realization of what had happened was just now affecting him. *I could have tried to escape*, he thought. *Why didn't I? Why did I help Candra?*

"Please give me the Tazor, Eric," Nathan said strongly.

Blinking, Eric looked slowly at the Tazor and then up at Nathan. The indecision showed in his eyes. He looked at Candra. He remembered their talks at the stream, their time with Gran, the help she had been to him while he was hurt. He was a Prince of Tolden--trained to hate and kill Unidans. Unidans were crazy and good only for the fields or to Raid.

But they don't know I am a Prince of Tolden, Eric thought. *And I don't want them to know*. Eric made his choice, slowly turning the Tazor handle towards Nathan. He did not notice that Handen had been standing behind him and was now returning his own Tazor to its sheath.

"Here, Nathan," he said, slumping to a heap on the log seat. Candra ran to him, stooped in front of him and laid her hands on his knees. With an effort to keep from crying, she exclaimed, "Eric! You saved my life. She was trying to hurt me. And you could have tried to escape. What does all this mean?"

"It means, Candra, The Beloved One, that I love you. I want to stay here with you and know your One and the Cause."

Candra did not know what to say. They looked into each other's eyes for a long moment. The veil was gone from Eric's eyes and Candra could see into his soul. Surprise filled her eyes and a little fear. A Tolden--loving her and looking at her like that? "I need to be alone," was all that Candra could manage. She stood and turned to walk along the path towards the stream. Nathan followed her, waiting at a distance until he could see that she was ready to talk it through with him-- her First Companion. Eric's eyes followed after her as they so often had while he was ill.

Watching the two, Handen spoke first to The One in his heart, then he turned to watch his daughter's retreat. The test of her training was plainly upon her. She knew the ways of The One about taking a Last Companion. Would her training outweigh her feelings? Walking over to Eric, Handen laid his hand upon the young man's shoulder, seeing the distress on his face. "Come, My Son. Let us talk. It is a giant gulf you stand before. The One will meet you."

Eric stood, looking at Handen with a mixture of gratefulness and apprehension. Together they walked to Handen and Esleda's tent.

CHAPTER TWELVE

At home inside her tent, Gran gently cleaned and anointed the bruised spot on Brinid's hand. She was nursing a more subdued Brinid. "There now," she soothed, "it wasn't too bad. The young Tolden did not chance the burning light. You could have fared worse."

"How is it that you can sit there and mend my hand when I have just tried to hurt your granddaughter?" asked Brinid. "You must be as crazy as Lornen."

"The love that is in my heart for you, Little One, is not about what you do or have done. The love is for who you are."

"How can you know who I am," mumbled Brinid, "when I don't know myself?"

"You are a child of The One and that is enough for me," answered Gran.

"I know not this one you speak of," said Brinid, lowering her eyes from the kindness in Gran's.

"Yes, I know," she said, gently lifting Brinid's chin, "But He knows you, My Love, and that is what counts. He alone can tell you who you are, define you, teach you."

Unwanted tears were welling in Brinid's eyes as she looked at Gran. "Long, so long, have I wished to know who I am. The last few weeks have made me tired. Nothing makes sense anymore. Unidans who treat me well-- even when I try to hurt their loved ones? I am allowed to wander the camp, never searched for a weapon, accepted just on Lornen's word. No one has pushed me, yet all have pulled me with kindness. I'm so tired of fighting and being angry." Brinid lowered her head. "You say there's another way? How can I believe you?" she continued with a bit of the old resistance in her voice. "It's easy for you to say."

"You can believe her, Brinid, "said Lornen, quietly walking over to touch her shoulder. "When you are ready to hear, you will hear. The One is real--the only real there is. He speaks and pulls you even now--to acknowledge Him--to take Him as your life. What you have been feeling from us that you do not yet understand is how much He loves you. "

Gran lifted up Brinid's face with a gentle hand and looked directly into her eyes, "The life you have always sought and longed for, Dear Brinid, is not to be found in the city. It is not even found here in our camp. It is only to be found in Him."

Brinid sat silently engrossed in deep contemplation. She had braved the hard life for as long as she could remember. She had fought hard to stay alive, worked hard to have her freedom. Could it be true that she could give up and let go? Could she let another be responsible? "But he is invisible," she barely murmured aloud.

"Is He invisible, Brinid? Have you not already seen Him? Here in Lornen? Nathan? Candra? The others?"

"Perhaps you are right, Old One. I will consider your words. What must I do about the one I tried to injure? What will she do?"

"That is between you and her," answered Lornen. "Wait for tomorrow and see. Are you ready to return to our tent, or do you wish to be here tonight with Gran?"

"I will stay here for the night. Maybe she will tell me more of her world." Brinid suddenly gasped, jumping frantically to her feet, "My knapsack! Oh, where is it? I forgot it! It must be by the tree!"

"I will get it for you," Lornen said opening the tent flap. When he returned, Brinid snatched the bag from Lornen's hands, clutching it tightly to her chest. Lornen and Gran exchanged a glance as Brinid dropped back onto the cushions, curled into a ball, and fell into an exhausted asleep.

# # # #

Candra was alone at her favorite spot by the stream. There the creek bed dropped down with a shallow pool at the bottom. In the good years the drop was a beautiful cascade and a deep pool, but today there was only a trickling, quiet waterfall dripping into an almost empty hole. Her thoughts were anything but quiet. First of all I have almost been killed today--and not by a

Raid but in my own camp. Then a Tolden declares his love for me. For the next while, Candra spent time speaking with The One Within, struggling with bad thoughts towards Brinid and fearful ones about Eric. As she finished sorting her feelings and opened her eyes, Nathan came through the trees where he had been patiently waiting. "I thought I would find you here," he said softly. "As your First Companion I come to speak truth with you. How comes the light?"

"I have spoken with The One." Candra answered without looking up. "I know His words. But Nathan, it is so hard right now. Two Toldens in the camp--two problems. One hates me; one loves me." Taking hold of her brother's hand as he sat down beside her, Candra looked at Nathan with a flicker of anger. "I know the words about forgiveness that we have been taught and that I should forgive the Tolden girl. But she tried to kill me! It's all so confusing. Nothing like this has ever happened here, only in raids, out there," Candra pointed across the creek to the woods beyond the camp.

"I don't think your anger and hurt are wrong, Candra," her brother said quietly. "Forgiveness has been easy for us all these years, as everyone here practices it so readily. Remember our pledges on your Becoming Day?"

Briefly a smile crossed Candra's lips as she looked at her brother. "Yes. Which part?"

"We pledged many things, but the principle thing, I think, was that we would say the truth to one another and help one another prepare for living with our Last Companion. The Elders say that how we relate to each other in conflict is very important, right? And the closer we relate, the more we have to rely on The One. That's even truer in times of conflict when we are hurt. He knows that we can't help but feel our hurts at first. We shouldn't push them away, but then we need to come to forgiveness, to finish the cleansing. This hurts you more than anything since losing Grandfather Wilden, doesn't it?"

Candra sat very still as Nathan's words settled on her heart. There were so many new feelings to sort through these days. Nathan watched her face. He could see there was a struggle and that it cost her as she heard the truth. Her brow relaxed a little as the struggle grew lighter. "Thank you, Nate. I do hear you. Gran told me a few weeks ago that all this is part of my learning since becoming a Participant. I have known these words from my cradle and watched the Elders as they handle many things, but this is definitely taking me deeper into a better understanding of the words of The One. I am being called to love in a way like I have never had to before. It was easy here in Unidan with you, Father and Mother, Gran always loving me. But now--to love a Tolden girl who tries to kill me—that feels impossible!"

"Yes, Candra," he whispered softly. "Yes it is. That is the thing we must keep remembering!" The love in Nathan's eyes supported the words pouring from his heart, encouraging Candra as she watched him draw from The One to speak the truth with her. He continued, "*His* love for an enemy is the only love that will work and, really, it's His love even when it's easy because it's for each other. Remember how Gran always says, 'His love is in you. How you let it come forth is your choice?'"

"I remember," Candra whispered, thinking about the last time Gran reminded her of that truth.

Nathan warmed to her response and continued. "You and He are One, Candra. This makes His love your love. Your part is to believe that and then choose to let it come forth from Him through you. Know that if He loves her--so do you. Because He forgives, you can, too. He is your very life and by faith He walks it out through you."

"Oh, Nathan, it seems so simple and yet feels so hard." Candra began to cry and Nathan reached out to hold her close to his chest. From deep inside, her tears and groans came forth to release her from the fear and hurt of being attacked. The One Within was comforting her, too, as she pictured herself sitting on His lap. This helped her take the truth and allow it to settle deeply into her heart. Nathan echoed His words aloud, "It's alright to feel this way. It hurts to be attacked. You can take your time."

A few moments later Candra dried her face on her sleeve, sat up, and with her head bowed, whispered, "Thanks, Nate. I do know you're right. I love The One and His ways and truths. He is my life. I want Him to show His love in me, even to this Tolden girl. I will talk with her tomorrow." As she looked up at her brother, she felt unsettled again as she remembered Eric. "And the other Tolden? What about him?"

"You must continue to walk that out, Candra. Give it time and you know The One will make it clear to you. His words do not speak quite as clearly of these things as they do of forgiveness and love. Just keep on moving ahead one step at a time. I will be here to listen when you need a human voice and ear."

"And . . . did you notice?" Nathan ended, his tone changing back to the fondly remembered younger brother. "She's a girl, not a boy

"Yes, Brother, I saw she's a girl. I can see that you're going to have to be patient and walk out some of your own feelings the same as I will," she said with a laugh, hugging her brother, her First Companion. Candra relaxed into a gentle wave of relief and comfort. Nathan was back to awaiting the next adventure. Together they stood and began walking back to the camp.

CHAPTER THIRTEEN

While having their breakfast with Esleda the next morning, Candra and Nathan told her of their conversation about the Tolden girl. Their mother's love and wisdom confirmed their talk by the stream as she encouraged them both to keep listening to The One. Esleda could see that Candra was peaceful about forgiving the girl's attack. "Go in faith," Esleda said as she touched her daughter's cheek, "that she will have some explanation of her actions and that she will hear your words as being from The One. We know nothing of what her life has been. Obviously Lornen sees her through the eyes of The One. Let's anticipate why The One had Lornen bring her here."

"Thank you, Mother," Candra said humbly. "Your support is very important to me and your reminders about how bad it can be in Tolden help me to focus. I know you will speak to The One on my behalf as I go." Candra hugged her mother as she rose to her feet from the pillows and motioned to Nathan to follow. "Come on, Nate. I want to find Father and see Gran, too."

The two young people hurried to Gran's tent hoping to find their Father there. Opening the tent's flap, they were surprised to also find Eric sitting there on the cushions near the fire, with Brinid sitting as far away as she could get inside the small enclosure. "We thought you two would be alone," Candra said hesitantly before entering, but Gran's smile welcomed them in.

Brinid, her black braids freshly done and securely pinned back, kept her head bowed over her bowl while she ate.

Upon seeing her, Nathan stammered out his thoughts again, "A girl. Well, what do you think about that," At this, Gran and Candra began to laugh out loud, breaking the heavy tension in the air.

"A very beautiful one, too, I will say," answered Gran. "Her name is Brinid." Hearing this Brinid blushed but still did not lift her head.

Nathan and Candra greeted their father and Eric. Candra found it difficult to look at Eric, until she saw the eager smile on his face. "Your father and I came to tell Gran about our talk last night. I received The One Within, Candra."

Candra, though not completely surprised, was at the same time not sure what to think of it all. Everything was happening so quickly. "I rejoice with you, Eric," she smiled shyly as he rose from the cushions to stand with her. "It is the most important thing in the world--to have Him within. There is nothing in the world more valuable."

"I have something else very important to tell you. May we talk later?" Eric asked hopefully, reaching to touch her hand.

"Yes," Candra answered, glancing first to their hands then at Eric. She did not draw back. She stole a look at her Father before saying. "I will find you when I am finished here." Eric turned to leave, giving Gran a hug as he left. Candra knelt beside of Brinid.

"We must talk," Candra said with soft strength, addressing herself to the girl. "It's difficult, but it is our way. The One wishes us all to be as He is—

loving, forgiving and not divided." Then she took a breath before asking a little more firmly, "Why did you try to kill me?"

"I wished only to get your Tazor so I could escape," replied Brinid, eyes still fixed on her bowl.

"I don't believe that." Candra countered softly. "You could have tried to steal a Tazor some other way. Instead you attacked me with your Sedat."

Brinid raised her head. All the years of pain and anger suddenly rose to the surface. Her beautiful green eyes flashed and she clenched her fists. With quickened breath she spat, "Because I hate you and all your people! All my life I have known deep down inside that Unidans caused me to be alone. I've listened to the talk in Tolden about the things you people do and how you are hated. I've felt the hatred that kind of talk stirs. Because I'm alone I've had to roam the streets eating garbage, sleeping where I could. Once I found a place to live, but the people there abused me." Memories poured through her mind, and Brinid could not seem to stop them. Now she had new ones coming that she had never let herself remember before. She screamed with agony and cried, "I hate you! I hate you! I hate you!"

She put her hands to her face, letting tears fall that she had so long denied. Her shoulders shook uncontrollably with the sobbing as Candra, Nathan and Gran waited silently. After a few minutes, Gran quietly came to sit beside the grieving girl and reached out her hand to touch Brinid on the arm. When she saw no resistance, Gran gently drew the wailing girl into her arms. Still sobbing, Brinid relaxed into Gran's arms. For the first time since she could remember, someone was helping her bear the pain.

Slowly the sobs turned to sniffs. Gran whispered kindly, "You are not alone any more, Daughter. Your tears are cleansing. They help bring the way for total healing and for knowing who it is you really hate. Healing will help you find what you seek."

Everyone in the tent remained quiet, patiently feeling Brinid's pain with her. Sobs began anew as Brinid murmured through her tears, "I don't know what I seek. How can I? I don't even know who I am."

Gran waited another moment before addressing the cry. "*That* is what you hate, Dear One, not us. It's your own self--and all that has happened to you. You seem to believe somewhere deeply that you are the problem, that something is wrong with you because you're alone."

"Of course, I am the problem" Brinid sobbed, her head on Gran's chest. "No one wants me. No one loves me. No one even knows who I am." Brinid's words were ripping Nathan's tender heart while he listened as her deepest fears came out. He wanted to help, but knew the best way was to remain quiet and speak inside to The One on Brinid's behalf. A look of understanding passed between Nathan and Candra as they watched Gran talk to the hurting girl.

Gran reached down and took Brinid's chin in her hand. Slowly she lifted the now blotched face, swollen from so much crying and looked deeply into the teary eyes, "*We* know, Love."

The tears stopped in surprise. Brinid stared at Gran, then turned and looked with amazement at Candra and Nathan and Handen. "You know?"

Handen was the one to answer this question, with his strong but kind voice. "You belong to The One. He wants you to believe Him and take Him for yourself. He will fill you with Himself, heal your wounds and show you who you are," he told the puzzled girl.

"Oh, I do so want to know, more than anything. I've been wanting to know for so long," Brinid said with longing as she wiped her wet face on her sleeve. "I want to understand why I was left on the streets alone; who I am! I want to remember my life."

"First you must know Him and learn about yourself in Him," Gran continued. "He holds our past and our future, and He is our peace in the present." Gran sat very still, watching the green eyes take in what they were saying. She saw hope, then fear of more unknowns, and finally relief wash over Brinid's face.

"I want to believe you," Brinid sighed. She couldn't take her eyes off of Gran, couldn't pull away from such a kind and understanding face. Finally she let down her guard. "I've been fighting to live all my life. I'm tired-- very tired. I see in you all here something that touches me and gives me hope." Mustering a little confidence, trying to be brave, she went on. "But I'm frightened. It all sounds like it is too good to be true. And," she said suddenly dropping her gaze, "You don't know how bad I've been."

Gran was moved by the shame in Brinid's voice. "You're no different than the rest of us," she assured softly. "We all came to The One realizing how bad we really were without Him. But The One takes care of that badness for those who receive Him. He will forgive you and change you completely. He will give you His very own life and live out of you from within." Gran waited for Brinid to look up before she finished. As Brinid dared to raise her eyes, Gran's voice became stronger, wanting to be certain that the girl understood. "Then you might do bad things, but your true self in Him will no longer be bad. Who you are, Brinid, and what you do are two very different things."

"How can He love me like that? How would I ever repay Him?"

"He desires for you to know and follow Him, Brinid," Gran assured the still puzzled girl. "When you understand He is your life from within, it will be much easier to follow Him and live as He wants you to live. There is no re-payment, Brinid, as His gift of Life to you is free. Then the living will not be left up to you, but up to Him through you. Who you are and what you do are two very different things."

Brinid looked up at Gran, not quite understanding the words that Gran had repeated, but trying to find assurance that she was speaking the truth. Gran's gaze never wavered, waiting for Brinid's next question. It came as Gran expected. "How do I know this one?"

"You simply decide to believe that He is The One, that He wants you and will be in you as your life forever," Gran replied. "It is His part to forgive all your wrongs and heal your wounds. Then He can teach you many things about life."

Brinid looked down again. She sat very quietly for a moment, her face mirroring what was going on in her heart. When she looked back up at Gran, this time her green eyes shone with peace and determination. She glanced at each one there in the tent and said strongly, "I take The One for my life and will let Him teach me the rest." Then with a deep sigh, Brinid finally relaxed upon Gran's chest, and allowed herself to be enfolded in loving arms.

The girl opened her eyes a few moments later as Candra touched her hand. "Brinid." The tearstained eyes looked up. "I forgive you," Candra said lovingly. "This is His way--bringing people together--within themselves and with others as well."

Brinid sat up earnestly and faced Candra. "I am truly sorry, Candra. I have never felt sorry about anything until now, much less said the words. I am very, very sorry that I took out my anger and hurt on you. Thank you for forgiving me."

"I do. And The One has made it well between us," answered Candra, smiling as she held out her arms for a hug. After the two girls hugged, Candra turned to her brother with a laugh, "Nathan, have you yet found your tongue to say something besides, 'She's a girl?'"

Nathan squirmed and laughed. "All I have to say is, 'What a girl!' Now I have another sister. Welcome to the family of The One, Brinid. Welcome home." With that, Nathan rose to leave, giving Gran a quick kiss on the cheek and tapping each girl on top of the head. "I still have chores to do today. I will see you ladies in the evening, and you, Father," he added with a big grin as he left the tent. It was now Nathan's turn to sort through his feelings.

Brinid rose and reached for her knapsack in the corner, needing to wipe her face. Candra hugged Gran and prepared to leave. Having passed Nathan just outside, Lornen appeared in the doorway. "Good morning, Dear Ones. And have we worked through yesterday's trouble?"

"I think so, Lornen," answered Candra as she and her father rose to leave at the same time. "Gran and Brinid can tell you all about it. I must go, too." Handen nodded in agreement as he and Candra passed Lornen at the entrance.

Lornen came in and sat down on the cushions near Brinid. Gran gave him some hot tea. They exchanged a glance behind Brinid as she felt inside her knapsack for a cloth. Then Gran nodded to Lornen. "Brinid," Gran started, "we know a little more of who you are than what you have just learned — being a child of The One."

"What?" Brinid exclaimed, dropping her knapsack. "You know what?"

"I have seen a glimpse of the treasure you hold in your knapsack," said Lornen.

Brinid grabbed it quickly, clutching it to her breast, her eyes frightened once again. "It's mine and no one else's. No one else knows. How do you know?"

Gran rose and slowly walked over to the small chest in the corner. She raised the top and reached inside, gently drawing out a skin pouch. While Brinid watched, Gran slowly unwrapped the package in her hand, removing a folded parchment exactly the color of Brinid's.

"You took it while I slept!" she accused, nearly in tears again. "You said you loved me. How could you? It's all I have."

"Brinid," Gran responded softly, touching the girl's shoulder as she sat down beside her again. "It is not as you think. You will learn trust and patience... and that we mean what we say." Gran's hands moved reverently as she continued unfolding the parchment. Laying it before Brinid, she looked into the girl's shocked face.

Brinid looked at Gran and then at Lornen. They saw her face change from shock and anger to confusion. There was nothing left for her to do but look inside her knapsack. She opened it and put her hand inside. She felt the prize under her fingers and pulled it out. Her piece wasn't stolen! It was right here. Then what was this? Yes! She could see a difference, as she took a closer look. She opened her half of the parchment and laid it beside the other. The jagged edge that she had looked at and touched so often fit perfectly with the jagged edge of the other.

Gran could hardly keep back the tears. To think that she was sitting here looking at the whole parchment reunited in her lifetime. She had hoped to live to see this day, but had wondered if it would ever come. Lornen held his breath, staring at the two women. Brinid broke the silence with a gasp, "What...who...what...?" was all she could get out.

CHAPTER FOURTEEN

Lornen and Gran had gone all around the camp, rejoicing over the miracle of both Brinid and Eric finding The One and then, finding the other half of the parchment. Candra needed to be alone with The One. She sat in her tent for a while, and then found her way back to the stream. She was looking for Eric, supposing he had returned to their favorite place. The time she had spent alone in her tent had helped Candra put the pieces together, and she was beginning to realize that the One's plan was unfolding before her eyes. The realization was freeing her to explore her real feelings about this

Tolden who had come to know Him and her people. "Hi, Eric," she said softly. I thought I might find you here." Approaching the large rock where he was sitting, her face brightened enthusiastically as she continued, "Did you hear the news? Brinid has come to The One. And, she is the one who holds the other half of Gran's parchment. Lornen caught a glimpse of it the other day when she was returning it to her knapsack."

"Yes, I did hear." Eric answered with equal excitement. "Nathan told me. What a great thing for your Cause! What will happen next?"

"This calls for a Council meeting to decide what to do. I hope Father will allow me to go to the Dome with the first group when it is arranged," she chattered as she plopped down beside Eric.

"Your Father told me many things about your people. It's not all clear, but I do want to understand. You are all very different than most of the people in my city."

"Are there other Toldens like you, Eric?" Candra questioned curiously, changing the subject. "You seemed so different, even before knowing The One, than I thought a Tolden would be."

"Many of the ordinary people wish to live in peace, Candra, but not so many in the Court. There was one," Eric said sadly, "but she died some time ago."

"What do you know about the Court?" Candra questioned him again as she searched his face.

"I know that the King is very evil and cruel. I know he hates the Unidan people and captures them and uses them any way he can for his own comfort, causes or entertainment."

"What about his family? Does he have any children to carry on his evil after he dies?" Candra probed.

Eric had known since his talk last night with Handen that he had to be completely honest with Candra the next time he saw her. He remembered Handen's encouragement to trust the One Within. "Yes. He does. He has two sons, twins."

"What are they like?"

"They are as different as day and night, Candra. One is evil like his father and cruel to his younger brother. Neither the father nor the older brother cares what happens to the younger one. All of Tolden knows who the next king will be."

"You seem to know much about these sons, Eric. Were you part of the Court or just a soldier?" Candra waited anxiously for these replies, seeing the struggle in Eric's eyes to find the right words.

"I was part of the Court. I saw firsthand the evil there. I was trained and ready for Raids on Unidan. The treatment of captured Unidans was horrible, especially when they were sent to the ring for sport, but I was too afraid to say what I thought. People who disagree with the King are not around very long." Candra could see the pain Eric now felt about his own participation as a Tolden in the fight against her people.

"Did Father help you last night with those things you're ashamed of? This is part of what it means to know The One, to know His forgiveness."

"Yes. It was a huge burden of guilt lifted from my heart. It helped to tell your father, too. He did not condemn me. He knows all about me now, as I want you to." It was very difficult for Eric to look at Candra. She could see the tension in his body as he rose from the large rock to pace in front of her.

"What else is there to know, Eric?" she asked quietly. "It's alright. You can tell me." Candra waited, patiently watching the resolve and apprehension flash across his face.

After a few moments, he looked directly into her eyes. "I am the King's son, Candra. I am the Second Prince of Tolden."

Candra sat very still, holding his gaze. She was overwhelmed with feelings: sadness that Eric was not loved by his father and brother; apprehension that this man loved her and it was beginning to dawn on her that she loved him back; wonder at The One's power in their lives. Candra knew she could trust The One. She shook her head and spoke, "I think it is alright with me, Eric. Maybe I was not completely surprised. You have a way about you that is not ordinary."

Eric sat down with a sigh, greatly relieved to have everything out in the open. *This is much better than hiding, not as frightening as I'd feared.* With a grateful heart he assured Candra, "I know you may need more time to think and more time with your parents and Gran, but I will wait for you as long as it takes. I love you, Candra. I want to be your Last Companion and learn all that means. I want to become one of your people."

2006 Barbara Moon

Candra took Eric's hand. She looked into Eric's eyes, trusting the One to keep her steady, though her heart was touched to tears. "Besides our Cause here in Unidan and Brinid's Parchment, I have been thinking of little else, Eric. I must be alone to ponder and talk to the One." Squeezing his hand as she rose to leave, she smiled through tears welling up in her eyes and murmured softly, "We will continue to talk to Him and I want to talk more with you."

CHAPTER FIFTEEN

Two days quickly sped by after the revelation of Brinid's parchment. Excitement spread throughout all of Unidan, bringing work to a standstill as everyone discussed and rejoiced over the news. Was it finally possible to see an end for The Cause--peace on Atron and an end to the drought? With both parchments now in hand, someone could be sent to find the Dome--the Books--the ancient secrets of the Universe. With the Books surely the Toldens would finally understand and come to know The One, bringing about peace and unity. What could be more wonderful!!

Thankfully, Candra's favorite spot by the stream was away from all this chatter. She needed a place where she could think. A person of action, she sat pensively formulating a plan. With everything in place Father had to allow her and Nathan to search for the Dome. All her life she had waited for this moment, hoping but not knowing if it would ever materialize. She was going to ask him tonight.

"Candra? Are you there?" she heard Eric's voice through the bushes.

"Eric!" she answered. "Yes. Come. Sit. I've been lost in thought about what has happened the past few days. It all still seems like a dream! Both Parchments here in our hands! I can hardly get my mind to rest for thinking of the possibilities of finding the Dome. I'm glad that Father and Gran told you and Brinid more about everything."

"Do you think your father will allow you to be part of the journey? He has never let you go past The Edge and nobody has been into The Beyond."

"I must be part of it! I have to go! Every day since I can remember I have dreamed of this time. I will ask him tonight. He has to say yes," she said reassuringly.

"Well, I am with you whatever arises," Eric said taking her hand. He looked into her eyes for a brief moment. There he found a fire of intent to find the Dome, and, something else--the flash of uncertainty at his gesture.

"Thank you, Eric," she answered but did not remove her hand. "Since understanding The One as your life, you are becoming as one of us."

"I want it to be more than that, Candra," he smiled. " I want to be as one with you."

With lowered eyes Candra sighed deeply. "I am frightened, Eric, of all that means. You know how we are taught about our Last Companion. It's very important to be sure. It is a huge decision."

"I will wait. Every day I am learning and appreciating your people and their teachings more and more. We will know." Jumping up and taking her other hand, he said, "Come on. Let's go back to the Square. Everyone is still out there talking about what is to come."

# # # #

After dinner in their parents' tent, Candra and Nathan glanced tentatively at each other as they readied themselves to approach Father with their request. Handen relaxed on the pillows as Nathan and Candra cleaned the bowls in the bucket of fresh water. After taking a big gulp of air, Candra burst out," Father. I want to go on the search for the Dome."

"And I also, Father," Nathan jumped in before Handen had time to react. "You surely must let us go! We have waited for this to happen all our lives!"

"Are there not others who have waited much longer, My Children?" he answered softly without opening his eyes. "There is much to be considered. Candra has but eighteen summers, and you less Nathan. All cannot go. We must keep Unidan safe. Someone has to continue running the grain and getting news from Tolden." Handen turned onto his side towards his expectant children, just barely coming out of his nap. "There are many things important to our Cause."

"Oh, Father, anyone can do those things," pleaded Candra. "We just have to go. We couldn't bear to be left behind to wait." Both young people knelt beside their drowsing father. Their mother watched as the young people continued pleading their case. She spoke quietly inside to The One, petitioning His wisdom for her husband, giving Him her own fears for what Handen might decide to do.

"There are dangers in The Beyond that we don't know about, Daughter. No one still living has been into the forest past our boundary and that of the

Tolden's." Handen opened his eyes to look at his beloveds in their distress and passion.

"Father," the two continued pressing their case, "We've both been trained and have our Tazors. We have The One," Nathan reminded him. "We're Companions! We're Participants!"

"I am sorry, but I have to say no," Handen said, reaching out to pull them close to his heart. "I cannot allow you to go on the initial journey. After the way is found, you can be the next to go. There will be many journeys made to the Lost Dome with much studying of the Ancients' ways in order to restore Atron and her people to all that they once knew. You young ones," he continued with a squeeze, "are the future of Atron. You will be the ones to reunite Tolden and Unidan. I cannot chance losing you."

Esleda felt some relief at Handen's decision, but her heart was with the young ones' deep desire to follow their Cause. Once she too had been a Participant. She remembered the burning within her own heart to see this day come. And now it was here. Esleda knew that she and Handen could not go on the first journey and would have to remain behind to lead and protect the camp. With faith and peace, she rested in The One, saying nothing. Having given his answer, Handen lay back onto the cushions to doze once again.

Candra and Nathan stared at the floor, and then looked up at each other. They knew when their Father spoke he meant what he said. Their training was not only in the use of the Tazor, but also in obedience to the Elders.

They returned to tidying the tent, each feeling what the other was thinking. Never had they disobeyed since a young age. It seemed impossible even to consider, but they both were doing just that. As their father quietly dozed, Candra and Nathan spoke to one another with their eyes. The temptation to disobey this particular decision from their father was very strong in both of them. Sister waited for brother. Brother waited for sister. Neither spoke. Inside, the Truth was quiet and still, but present, as this very real but invisible battle with the Tempter was taking place. All their lives they had been waiting for this very day. Scarcely had any other thing been discussed as often in their presence. Their longing to participate was palpable.

Candra, the first to break the silence, groaned with anguish, "I cannot. I cannot. I feel the pull of defiance, but I can't! Though this decision feels so unfair, I still must trust Father's leadership here. The One is too real! The teachings about obedience are too true to do anything else."

"My sister, my Companion, I too felt it. It seemed alive and real, almost touchable! Not like anything I've yet experienced!" Nathan was stunned at the power and aliveness of the temptation. "Father, Father! Wake up!" he cried as he rushed back over to Handen's dozing form. "We almost were drawn to defy you and the Council and find a way to go on the journey," Nathan babbled as the startled Handen jerked from his sleep.

"What! What is it, My Son?"

"Father," Candra took up the cry as she knelt beside them, "we want to go so badly that we were almost drawn into going without your permission. The pull was so strong . . . like it was alive. We both felt it. Help us, Father. We do not wish to disobey." Candra dropped her head onto his chest sobbing as Handen lifted his hand and placed it lovingly on her head. The other hand went out to Nathan, drawing them once again into his embrace.

"My Children, I feel your struggle. I hear your pleas. Remember, The One is stronger than the Tempter. The One is your keeper. You only need to listen and be in touch with Him inside." Handen was quiet, patting Candra and looking into Nathan's eyes, as his son's head rested on the strong shoulder. Handen's face became pain stricken as some inner wrestling began to take place deep in his own heart. He closed his eyes, as all three remained quiet. Esleda watched and talked to The One.

At last Handen broke the silence. "Perhaps I have spoken too quickly, My Children, and from my father's heart before listening within. I was seeing you only as my children, forgetting that you are also warriors for our Cause." Handen glanced over at *his* Companion, seeing the peace in Esleda's eyes, he read her heart. She nodded as he continued, "The One is telling me that you both are to go and that I must trust Him with it." Candra remained very still on his chest as he continued, "Because the future of Atron is yours and those of your generation, you must go. We have trained and taught you well for this very moment. I cannot keep it from you. You shall have it."

As Candra looked up, brushing the tears from her cheeks, her smile matched that of her brother's. Their eyes were bright as simultaneously they each threw an arm around the other and dived again onto Handen. "We're going! "We're going! Thank you, Father. Do you believe it? We're going!"

"Yes!" returned a joyful shout, "Yes! We're going!"

Untangling themselves from the cushions, the three sat up together, giddy with joy. Their mother, calm and sure, joined in their jubilation. Each parent, knowing the dangers and trials that could come with such an expedition, also knew that their children's hearts were filled only with the adventure that lay before them. Without the One, all would know only disaster. Candra and Nathan smiled humbly into the father's eyes, calmed by his strength and wisdom.

"The depth of your resistance to the Tempter has blessed me," their father spoke. "That encourages me that you are ready for this task. For this and other tests to come, I speak a blessing of The One's strength upon you both. Only He knows what is ahead and only He can guide you through the ways that He leads."

"As the Council continues to consider The One's directions, He will show us the details for the plans that need to be made. Go now and share with Gran what has happened here tonight. It is time for me to go the Council meeting." Hugging each one in turn, both Handen and Esleda whispered, "I love you," and then pushed them gently towards the tent flap.

Hardly able to contain their excitement, Nathan and Candra ran quickly to Gran's tent. They found Eric and Brinid inside as they so often were, sitting with Gran, soaking up whatever she could share with them about the things of The One and the Unidan Cause. Sensing that something big was going on, Lornen left the garden where he was hoeing and followed close behind the two young people as they entered Gran's tent. They paused, just inside waiting for a moment to speak. Unable to keep quiet any longer, Nathan took a deep breath and interrupted with the news. "Gran, Father and Mother are letting us go on the expedition to the Dome!" As he and Candra knelt in front of the others on Gran's colorful array of pillows, everyone waited to hear the details of the surprise. Quickly Nathan and Candra told the story about their struggle to resist the Tempter, and then, how The One had spoken to their father, assuring him that he should allow them to go. "The Elders are meeting now," Nathan continued, "and will soon share the plan they receive from The One. Even now preparations are being made as they continue to carefully study the parchments to find all the clues."

Candra picked up the story as soon as Nathan paused. "Together they're deciphering the drawings and writings, even though it's so much harder because much of the Ancients' learning has been lost."

Grinning at his grandmother with his usual passion, Nathan continued with hardly a pause, "Gran! You're helping, aren't you?"

"Oh, yes, Adventurous One," she chuckled. "We are making progress. Having both halves together is helping us make more sense of the marks and is giving us a sort of map to the lost Dome. Part of the writing seems to be some kind of riddle that the travelers will have to unravel as they go. It is exhilarating and humbling to see The One at work here, bringing us closer to His plans for the Cause."

"Yes, He is working in many ways, Gran," Candra added, nearly bouncing with joy, "I can hardly believe we are going and that it's all coming true just as we'd all been hoping for so long."

"And you are the reason, Brinid," she smiled as she included the Toldens. "We interrupted your time with our exuberance," Candra apologized. "We cannot thank The One enough for bringing you here--for many reasons, not just the Parchment." What are you learning tonight?" she asked as she settled more comfortably into one of the huge pillows.

"Gran was preparing to tell us the history of the parchments and how I fit into it all," Brinid answered, her eyes filled with expectation. "For as long as I can remember I've been alone: sometimes living on the streets, always having to take care of myself. The only thing I knew was that my parents had been killed in some kind of a skirmish with the Unidans. I do not know anything else except that I was mistreated every place I went. I have told The One and Gran these bad things and they are helping me remember and find healing for it all."

"Brinid is helping also in the plans for our search for the Dome," reported Gran as she motioned for the Nathan and Lornen to join them on the cushions around her fire. "She knows Tolden territory well from her life on the move and she'll be able to help us travel around the Tolden territory, through the edges of the known forests, right into The Beyond. I've been waiting for Lornen to finish in the garden so that he could help me piece together the history that we do know concerning the parchments."

"Wait a minute!" interjected Nathan. "You mean Brinid is going with us?"

"Why yes, Nate," Lornen replied. She is an integral part of it all."

"I'm very glad," Nathan hurried to add with a big grin. "What about Eric? Who else is going? When do we start?" his questions tumbled out as his cheeks turned pink with embarrassment and excitement. It was becoming evident that Nathan seemed to stumble over his words when he was around Brinid.

"You will know the plans soon," Lornen said with a grin back at Nathan's apparent unease. "I can tell you Eric is going. We need four strong and brave young people to bolster the wisdom of the leaders. I truly thought that Handen would allow you each to go after he had some time to think it though and talk to The One. After all, you are the future of Atron," finished Lornen.

For a moment the group was quiet as each one considered the importance of the journey to the Dome. Candra was the next to speak as she prodded, "Go on, Gran. Go ahead and tell us what you know and how it fits." She had been listening quietly to the discussion, and with Eric sitting very nearby, she was also thinking about what he had said to her at the creek. It would be good to concentrate on Gran's story.

CHAPTER SIXTEEN

Glancing around the circle at each one of her young audience, Gran began. "This is the story I learned long ago about how it began. The earliest thing that anyone remembers is that there were two kings, Vandlyn and Brasald who were strong friends. Something happened to shatter their friendship. Both knew of the Origin of Atron and the work of the Ancients. They shared knowledge of the Dome and what it contains."

"Whatever happened between them caused jealousy and anger to drive them apart, though none of us knows exactly what that was. Most say that King Vandlyn was following The One Within and that the other, King Brasald had turned his back on The One and refused to follow Him again, refusing to listen to the pleas of his old friend."

"After this terrible rift in their friendship developed, Vandlyn took the Dome's electrokey, hid it and then made a map of its location in relation to the Dome. This map was the parchment now whole again, drawn to give clues to the hiding place of the electrokey, without which the Dome could not be opened."

"For some reason the good king, Vandlyn, felt an urgency to protect the Dome and its contents. He vowed to keep the parchment from Brasald's hands, guarding it with his life until his death. He would pass it to his heirs with the instructions to keep it safe until such a time that the people of Atron could be reunited. King Vandlyn realized that what once had been a deep friendship with Brasald had turned to hatred on Brasald's part. Vandlyn saw no way of restoring peace between their peoples, so he decided to travel away from the settlements to a new and different location. The directions to the Dome were added to the parchment in case the people should forget the way back."

Gran paused in her tale to sip some water from the clay jar at her side. She then continued, "Some of this, you Unidan young ones were taught, as we older ones were when young. The parts you don't yet know have always been kept for later revelation, when you become an Elder or a leader." Gran sipped again, almost lost in her own thoughts. She had always hoped such a time would come in her life, but it was still overwhelming to be watching it unfold.

The young listeners leaned forwards with expectation and awe, as Gran continued her story, "Brasald discovered that his former friend had hidden the electrokey and that there was a parchment map of its location. Anger rose up in him and so he plotted a strategy that would return the parchment to his kingdom and his own descendants. Vandlyn and his son, Damond kept the parchment in safe keeping among their own possessions, while they prepared to move their people to another part of Atron."

"Unaware that Brasald had quietly entered their dwelling with his Tazor drawn, prepared to kill them, father and son were slipping the parchment into its hiding place for safe keeping, when suddenly two blasts pierced the air from across the room. His aim true and quick, Brasald's Tazor blasts mortally wounded Vandlyn. Damond, still holding the unrolled parchment, turned swiftly, drew his Sedat and expertly wounded Brasald as he reached for the parchment. As Brasald grabbed for the parchment, he fell, tearing the parchment down the center."

"Still holding half of the now torn parchment, Damond sped away, fearing the wounded king might recover enough to catch him and take away his half of the parchment." Gran paused to catch her breath and to rest for a moment. "This is all we know of the story. Vandlyn's people moved through the forests of Atron until my grandfather Kolen's time. We have been here ever since."

"We know that Damond's family passed his half of the parchment down to his heirs, passing their version of the story along by word of mouth. We lost track of Brasald's half and how his people passed down the story and even how the two peoples came to live closely but in such disunity. We knew only that Brasald's descendants are the Toldens, who kept the monarchy and came to forget The One. As you most likely have figured out, Vandlyn and Damond's descendants are the Unidans, who follow The One as the Ancients did. We serve no king but Him."

No one could speak, each absorbing the story and its ramifications. Finally, Lornen broke the stillness that had settled around the tent. Calling Gran by name, he prompted, "Karand, tell them what we know about Damond."

"You tell that part, Lornen," Gran replied.

Lornen took up the story. "Damond learned well his lessons of the Ancients. Did he know the reasons for the broken friendship? We don't know, but we know this! He knew The One Within. Wherever he took his people, he taught them the things that have been passed down to us today. Gradually the two kingdoms split so cleanly that it was impossible to see they had ever been part of the same one. Gran's mother and her grandfather told her that there was another piece of the parchment and that it would lead to the Dome. We don't completely understand how it was all passed down to the present. We only know that the Ancients' Books are in the Dome and whatever the kings knew of the Origin of Atron is there. The drought is killing Atron, and so we feel hopeful there will be something in the Dome that will help us bring rain again."

The young people were still quiet. Each wondered what this story meant for them and what their part in the search might be. Brinid's eyes were averted from the others. Observing her silence and closed eyes, Lornen asked softly, "Brinid. What are you thinking, My Child?"

Tears began to fall from her eyes as she opened them to look up at the others. "Why did *I* have the Parchment?" she questioned Gran directly. "What does my having it mean?"

Gran responded slowly, allowing her wisdom and attunement with The One to form her words. "Are you beginning to see who you are, New One?"

"I am afraid to see it," her tears ran in a course down her face as she wept. Slowly she composed herself enough to whisper, "Please, say it for me." Brinid moved herself closer to Gran's side, drawing comfort from her stability.

"You're wishing you were not a Tolden anymore?" questioned Gran, gently putting an arm around her new child. "Does it feel terrible to you that you may somehow be an heir to such a cruel and violent king as Krall? Are you feeling ashamed, thinking that this means that you must be from his lineage and from Brasald's of old? Is it this that is causing you such pain?"

"All my life I have longed and searched to know who I am. Knowing all this, I feel so bad and frightened," Brinid said softly as she wiped her face. "Surely this cannot be who I really am! It's not fair!" The others watched as she struggled with the anger she had always used to protect herself in the past.

"Look at Eric," Gran instructed quietly, but firmly.

Opening her eyes and looking upwards, Brinid turned her face towards Eric. By the look on his face, Brinid could see that Eric felt just as upset with the story as she did. Gran nodded towards the young man, "Eric is the son of King Krall. Somehow, you and he are kin. You are part of his family. Do you think The One loves Eric and wants Eric to know Him and walk in His ways? Do you believe his roots have to determine who he is now?"

"Oh no, of course not! That couldn't be true for Eric. But for me? I don't think...." Her words faltered as she tried to accept the fact that she had a new beginning. It was hard to believe after so many years of never knowing that anyone loved and accepted her. Suddenly, Eric thought of a way to help her.

He moved closer to Brinid and tipped her chin to look up at him again. "Hello, Kinswoman," he whispered softly. "I love you and I welcome you to MY family."

As she absorbed the look in Eric's eyes, at last Brinid began to understand. The ever-present anger seeped away and she allowed herself to welcome his outstretched arms and, at that moment, accepted The One's love for her through Eric. The tears in her eyes began to flow freely again as the others joined them, forming an unbroken circle that served to multiply the love that Brinid had decided to accept.

Tired and happy, everyone finally settled back onto the cushions and Gran addressed Eric directly. "Eric, did you ever hear talk at Court about the short insurrection that happened several years ago?" Gran's words startled Brinid causing her to jump involuntarily.

"I have heard whispers now and then since I was a boy, but it is forbidden to speak about it." As Eric paused to pull up memories of what he had heard, the others were drawn to look at Brinid. Her body was bent and drawn, rocking back and forth. Moans oozing from her throat, she was a very sad sight to behold.

"Brinid!" exclaimed Candra and Gram simultaneously as Candra moved quickly to Brinid's side. "What is it? What's wrong?" She wasn't sure if she should touch Brinid or not.

Gran said tenderly, "I think she is remembering something terrible that happened to her. Let us ask The One to slowly show her and be her comfort as the memories come. You can go ahead and touch her arm or shoulder, Candra. It will help her know she is still with us and not alone."

Brinid's moans turned to cries. Everyone earnestly began talking to The One on her behalf. Candra touched her softly on the shoulder. After a few minutes, Brinid began talking between her sobs. "I am remembering the death of my parents, how they gave me the parchment when I was five or six winters old. I now remember them telling me that I was to guard it forever and never lose it. Something they were doing was very dangerous, but they would not tell me very much about it. I was too young. Your words brought it back to me--they were part of the insurrection against King Krall." Brinid began to rock again, holding herself tightly. Candra drew Brinid close as she put her arm around the suffering one's shoulder.

As her sobs subsided, Brinid continued to talk about all that was coming to her mind. "My mother was the sister of the queen-- your mother, Eric. They both felt the pain of knowing how evil the King had become. Your mother was very unhappy, and she suffered much as she watched the hardships your father inflicted on all the people, both Unidans and Toldens."

"A group finally rose up that wanted to overthrow the king and free the people from his tyranny. As this group planned and gathered help, my parents thought this might be the best way to safeguard the parchment. Fearing the worst, your mother had secretly given the parchment half to my mother. Though your mother was the real heir to the throne, King Krall had taken over and kept her from her true place as ruler."

"Your mother and mine were part of a group that had not totally rejected the rumors and some of the old stories about The One. The more evil King Krall became the more your mother feared even for her life. My mother was very sad for many days before the insurrection and it seems to me now that the king must have killed his own wife for her beliefs and to protect himself from her right to the throne."

Gran wisely interrupted as she saw the strain that remembering these painful events was having on Brinid. "Brinid needs to rest, My Children. Let us finish tomorrow when she has had some sleep. What do you say, Daughter?"

"I think I must finish this story now," she answered. "I want to get it all out. May I? Candra's nearness is giving me strength." She looked around at each of them. "Really, all of you are."

"Then continue, Dear One, and take as long as you need," Gran responded.

"All I remember about that horrible day of the insurrection is that my parents left to meet the others and never came back. I waited alone for them, hiding in a dark room, huddled into a corner. After a day or two, hunger drove me to a neighbor and his wife. All they could tell me was that the Unidans had killed my parents in a Raid. I was afraid to be alone again, so I went back and packed my knapsack with a few things and stayed with them. They were not sympathizers of the insurrection and after a while, the fear of someone coming for the parchment overcame my fear of being alone. I ran away and hid in the forest. I stayed there until hunger drove me back into the city."

"Much of what happened during that time and right afterwards was so awful, I guess I blocked it all from my mind until now." Brinid stopped to look at Gran. Gran could see the struggle going on inside the girl, but she could also see courage in Brinid's demeanor. Brinid spoke again, directly to Gran. "I want to tell you more of the details later when we are alone, Gran. Is that all right? I don't want the others to have to hear everything."

"Certainly, My Child," Gran reassured her. "Just tell whatever you want to now."

Encouraged by Gran's eyes filled with love and understanding, Brinid continued, "The parchment and a few belongings were all I had left of my life with my parents. I did not even know what the parchment was, but I knew at first that it must be very important if my parents died to keep it safe. I have never let it out of my sight. It is always with me in my pack, but through the years I forgot that it had any significance other than some kind of comfort to me."

"I learned to live on the streets and sometimes I was forced to live with bad people. I've been to the fields with your people. I took care of myself and trusted no one. The fear has kept me on the move ever since the first time I ran away; that is, until I found Lornen." Brinid took comfort from the beautiful smile that Lornen was sending her way. It touched her deeply to be accepted and loved by him and now by all the others. *Thank You, One, for my new life*, she breathed in her heart as peace began to settle over her. That peace was obvious to the others, as they watched her sink into the pillow against Candra's shoulder.

Eric was touched by Brinid's story. As everyone quietly shared her sadness, Eric was the first to speak. "Brinid, I hardly remember my mother at all," he responded softly. "Did your mother ever tell you anything about mine?"

The question was just what Brinid needed to help her return to the present. "I do remember something," she said brightly. "Your mother had a lady in waiting who loved her very much. Her name was Tylina. She listened to your mother's stories and wonderings; her troubles and her desires for change in Tolden."

"Tylina is who brought me up!" exclaimed Eric excitedly. "Wow! That explains why I am not like Stephad and my father! She must have been too frightened to tell me anything, but she often taught me to be kind and loving. Until she died she was always there when I had no one else."

Everyone began chattering at once as they all rejoiced and wondered aloud at all this new information. Pieces were coming together. Brinid had a family she could be proud of. Eric quietly thought about what Brinid had said, realizing that he now knew himself better and he could no longer wish to be like Stephad. Though it would be very difficult to be at war against his father and brother, these people sitting here around him would now be his new family and as he searched his heart, he found that this *was* where he wanted to be. He wanted to help the Unidans find the Dome and then seek ways to reunite Atron. Most of all he saw the deep desire in his heart to see the Toldens free and for them to have the opportunity to know The One. Maybe this would happen in his lifetime. For now, they would have to wait for the plans from the Elders and continue to make the preparations that would help them find the lost Dome.

He yet had much to learn from Gran and the others. And--there was this place of love in his heart to join with Candra for the rest of their lives. He was determined to show her that he could be worthy of her commitment. While he grieved over the truth about his father and brother, he could also sing with joy to The One for bringing him here to Unidan. He had never really fit as a prince of Tolden. In his heart he knew his destiny lay with these new friends who were fast becoming his true family.

Part Two: The Search for the Lost Dome

CHAPTER ONE

Using a translation of the newly restored parchment, Nathan, Candra, Eric and Brinid were now two days into their journey to find the lost Dome. Waiting to begin their journey had proven difficult. The Elders studied the parchment to decide how to send the first search party to the Dome. At the same time, Handen convened a special Council meeting to fully discuss making Eric and Brinid official Participants in their Cause. He had summed up how the Council felt about this move for the community: "We are delighted to welcome these two young people into our camp and our Cause before The One. We base our decision on the fact that their training in Unidan ways will continue as they live among us and grow with The One. We shall have their ceremony at a later date after we visit the Dome. But for now, we can call them 'Participants.'" Eric and Brinid smiled as the people of Unidan welcomed them with cheers of encouragement. Candra and Nathan, faces shining, stepped towards their new friends to give them a hug.

While waiting impatiently on the Council's leading about the search for the Dome, the young people continued to practice using Tazors and Sedats. They enjoyed becoming better acquainted and talked again and again of the miracles they had just experienced together.

Finally, the day came when the Elders had finished deciphering most of the parchment. The Elders then took some more time communing with The One. They needed His direction to choose ten others, who would lead, assist and protect the young people. Chregg, Handen's most trusted aide, was put in charge; though they would all would work together as a team under the direction of The One. A strong fighter and a wise leader, Chregg deeply trusted The One in all situations. His strength, gained from that trust, made him the perfect person for the young people to depend on during their upcoming journey. Tearfully, yet filled with faith and promise, the group set off toward the northern section of The Edge and then on to the Beyond. Brinid, serving as guide, led the eager group on a northeastern path far above the outside of the city, staying inside the cover of the forest, following the part of the Unidan map's directions that were faded and did not exactly match the other drawings. This section from the camp to the big river seemed to have been added at a later time.

On the fourth day, the search party found the river, far above the place it flowed on a southwesterly course near the Tolden fields. The water this river provided to their fields always made it possible for the Toldens to have more grain than the Unidans. For as long as they had heard talk about the river, it was said to be wide, deep and brisk as it ran through the Tolden territory. As children, each of the Unidans had played in the forest streams, though none of them had ever seen a large river like this one. Now standing at its bank, they could only imagine the river as it must have been before the drought. Though the banks were wide, today the river was shallow and narrow, a lazy stream instead of the mighty river it had once been.

While the Elders were planning the search party's journey to the Dome, they had discussed many methods of crossing the wide river. Serving as a boundary between civilization and the Beyond, it was unlikely that the area around the river this far north had ever been explored, since as far as they knew, no one had even crossed it close to the city. The Elders thinking the river would be low from the drought, still thought it deep enough to float a raft made of small logs. It was good to see their thoughts were valid.

The group set about the task of collecting logs, vines and mud for making the raft. They took a day to construct a sturdy raft at the edge of the water that would hold their supplies. "We can use this raft again when we return," Chregg suggested as they began piling their cloaks, blankets, weapons and other supplies on top of the small raft. "If we pull it up into the brush that lines the other side, it will save us some time coming back."

"Yes," said Marland, one of the scouts. "Crossing the river will be one obstacle we'll have to solve for our future trips to the Dome. I'll put that on my list of things to think about making for that purpose," she added. "The One has gifted me to see the ways of construction and I will be blessed to serve in that way."

"Your talent has already helped us build the raft," said her friend Jaren, one of the other scouts. "The way is easier as we share our gifts from The One, isn't it?"

At last they were ready to launch out across the water. The team swam along beside the raft, kicking and paddling as they propelled it gently across the slowly moving river, even walking part of the way along the pebbly bottom. They finally reached the other bank and pulled the raft up on the bank under some deep leafy brush. They were standing in The Beyond, on the far side of Tolden. They were truly dependent on The One for every step they would take as they followed the pieced-together clues from the parchment.

They began to make their way in this unfamiliar area with Brinid carrying the written instructions, translated by the Elders from the two halves of the parchment. This honor almost overwhelmed her. The Unidans' new love and her recent healing from The One had begun to transform her into the lovely, wonderful young woman Lornen had foreseen at their first meeting. She still struggled at times with feelings--fear, abandonment, anger--that had helped keep her alive when she was on her own, but her heart and mind were now fully occupied with learning about herself and relating to her new family. Her new friends were faithful to listen, attuned to her needs and brought her to The One and His truth. Having a family again, being accepted by people instead of running from them and then being chosen to go on this very significant journey was more of a gift than she could have ever dreamed having. She noticed in others like Marland, great joy in using their areas of giftedness and training to further The Cause. She yearned to discover and be able to use her own gifts from The One. *For now*, she thought, *the honor they've given me of carrying the instructions is enough.*

CHAPTER TWO

Stephad, First Prince of Tolden, stood silently at the foot of his father's bed. His evil life having now caught up with him, King Krall lay sick beyond all powers of herbs and remedies. His doctors stood nervously around his bed until the king ordered them away so that he could speak privately with his son. "Stephad, you must continue in my footsteps to bring ruin to the Unidans and keep them from spreading their tales here in our city. Allow only the ones you need for slaves to live within our borders. Tolden must rule." The king's voice had grown tired and raspy. He was barely able to speak.

Stephad chose not to tell his father of the rumor, spreading like wildfire throughout Tolden, that a band of Unidan rebels had just moved completely around the north of Tolden and walked right out into The Beyond. Having ordered his men to check out the rumors, he awaited their return. Stephad's desire to take over and take care of things himself completely overshadowed any sadness he might have felt about his father's critical condition. He assured the dying king, "I will do as you say, Father. You may go, knowing I will carry on your reign and bring an end to the division of Atron. Tolden will be the only kingdom of Atron when I am done!"

Stephad watched as the King closed his eyes and took his last breath. "At last I am King!" Stephad declared aloud. "I will go after that band of Unidans at once to see for myself why they dared venture past the edge of the known territory into the Beyond!"

CHAPTER THREE

The young travelers and their companions, having turned south as directed and now deep inside the outer territory, had been very surprised not to see anything very different on their journey. Leaves were falling to the ground everywhere they walked in the forest, branches drying much too soon for the season, another sign of the drought that held Atron in its deathly grip. Creeks barely trickled, game was scarce, bushes withered. Knowing they would be facing drought conditions, each Participant had brought, along with their weapons, as many supplies from home as they could. Yet even with all the supplies they had, they knew it would not sustain them for very long and they started looking for opportunities to replenish their stores along the way.

Each member of the chosen band carried in their pack a water jug, food, cooking or eating utensils, a change of clothes and a cloak.

In spite of dwindling supplies and the hardships and dangers they expected to find along the way, their spirits remained high as they traveled through the new territory. As they walked they took time to enjoy one another's company and discuss what they might encounter on the way in their search for the lost Dome. Eric and Candra often paired off as they walked, talking frequently about what Gran had shared with both of them. Trust and love grew between them, as Eric better understood the depth of commitment it would take to become Candra's Last Companion. Candra responded to one of his questions, "Being a Last Companion means deeply knowing each other in every way and it requires openness and honesty from both people. One cannot enter into such a commitment lightly, since it becomes a lifelong one." They also watched with whispered chuckles as Nathan and Brinid attempted to get better acquainted. Nathan had finally found his tongue and did not seem to get so flustered when he was around Brinid, as he had in the beginning.

After a time, the party emerged from the forest into a clearing that was scattered with large rocks and low brush. Their conversations were suddenly interrupted by the most piercing scream any of them had ever heard! Everyone stopped instantaneously as each one drew a Tazor or Sedat. "What!" Chregg asked quietly as he quickly motioned all the others behind the nearby rocks. "What was that?"

"I don't know," whispered Richen, one of the scouts, carefully gazing around the rocky section that stretched before them. "That sound is like nothing I've ever heard."

Candra was the first to see the creature, creeping out from behind a distant rock. "There!" she hissed carefully and pointed her finger to the right where a huge unfamiliar animal was stepping over each boulder as if it were a stone.

Covered with brown fur, the creature looked like some of the animals they hunted--except for its size. Advancing quickly toward them over the rocky terrain on four legs so large they looked like tree trunks, the creature let out another piercing scream. This time they could see its mouth--yellow teeth, fangs of death. Nostrils as large as small fruits flared as the creature sniffed out each of their hiding places. It would not greet them with a friendly hello.

"Set Tazors, Participants!" ordered Chregg. "One, we claim your power from within us that allows us to increase the blast," he spoke aloud, "and we fire as one on Your command!"

Well-trained and yielded to Him, the six Unidans armed with Tazors stepped from behind cover as one and blasted a deathly streak of energy focused directly into the creature's head. Stunned by the blast, it fell to the ground and became lodged between two of the larger boulders. "Fire again!" was Chregg's next call. This time everyone targeted the creature's chest, and the blast found more vital organs assuring the creatures death.

Seeing the body go limp, Chregg immediately sent some men to scout the area for other beasts, while others knelt to thank The One for His help and protection. Having just experienced her first battle as a Participant, Brinid looked down to find her Sedat clutched so tightly that her fingers were completely white. Arising and still shaking from their encounter with the beast, Brinid asked Nathan, "Do you think there are other creatures around here like that?"

"There have to be, I would think," Nathan answered taking Brinid's hands to help her gain composure. "Most creatures don't travel alone, though we can't be sure how old this one might be. If we don't find a way to end the drought, such creatures could venture closer to our settlements looking for food," he added as he drew Brinid a little closer, leading her towards the group where everyone was reassembling. "Another reason for our journey, huh?" he continued. "Don't forget, The One is leading and protecting us," he finished as they joined the others who were talking with the scouts who had returned to give their report.

"…none that we could see or hear," they were saying to Chregg. "Shall we move on to find another spot to rest or risk others coming if we take a chance and camp here?" Marland asked.

"Let's push on ahead to see if we might be able to find a place where we are out of range of any other such creatures. I think it best that we walk with Tazors ready, though," Chregg decided.

As the band slowly moved forward, picking their way carefully through the giant rock formations, they began to see a mountain in the distance. Awed by its height and anticipating what this meant to their quest, each heart was filled with joy. This mountain, familiar to each of them, was pictured on the parchment! "We are on the right path!" shouted Nathan, flashing his raised Tazor at the sky. "The Elders' translation is right! What a day!" Exhilarated, he picked Brinid up off the ground and twirled her around. They laughed together like two children.

"And," Candra reminded them all with even more glee, "the electrokey is hidden there!" The mysterious mountain rose high above them in the distance, looking as if it touched the very sky over Atron. "Again" she humbly reminded herself and the others, "we thank The One Within for guiding the Elders and protecting us!"

Smiling with the rest, Chregg said thoughtfully, "We shall camp just before the sun goes down. By then we should be close enough that we can make it to the mountain tomorrow." Atron's sun had moved below the trees when the weary men and women dropped their belongings to the ground beside a very small creek that was sparsely populated with a few scraggly trees. Now it was time to make camp. When they were finished, they ate lightly from their provisions and separated into two groups on each side of the fire pit, preparing for sleep. The girls, still somewhat shaken by the possibility of giant creatures roaming the area, talked with one another and the other women, Jaren, Joden, and Marland. Candra had always loved talking with Joden and she wanted Brinid to know Joden as well. Joden reminded them, "The One has sent us and knows all that will happen before it comes to pass. Perhaps when we find the Dome we will understand the huge beasts," she said. Around the glowing fire, the women spoke in quiet, reassuring tones until their feelings began to settle down and they felt the peace that comes from faith in The One

On the other side of the fire, a different sort of conversation was going on between Nathan and Eric. The young men found it easier to share with one another as the bonds first made back in the Unidan camp became stronger with each day of their adventure. Nathan and Eric found themselves discussing the girls. "I think I see Candra growing to love you more,"

Nathan encouraged his new friend with a gentle, teasing poke to Eric's side. "In Unidan, you know, we don't go only by the feelings we have for another. We have to know people well inside. Our desire is to be deep friends. But," Nathan continued meekly, "I will admit that it is very difficult not to go by feelings now that I've met Brinid." Eric chuckled at his friend's honesty as Nathan continued, "Ever since that first day when I watched her hood slip off and reveal her as she is, I have been thinking of little else but her and this journey."

"It helps me to hear you say that," Eric responded. "I'm glad that I'm walking the Unidan ways now. I have strong feelings for Candra and I know she is the person I want to spend the rest of my life with, but I trust The One to bring it to pass in His time. But, like you say, it's not easy to keep from daydreaming of that day." He looked ruefully at Nathan and returned his friendly jab.

"Perhaps this journey will reinforce the ways of The One in us all and then it should soon become clearer how things will come to pass," Nathan agreed wisely. "Of course I have to wait until my Becoming Day to act on my hopes. That's not easy either, but it gives more time to learn and grow." Nathan sank down into his blankets and said with a hopeful grin, "I know that I will greatly enjoy that learning time with her, if she agrees. Goodnight, My friend." Eric grunted his response as he pulled his cloak and blanket over his head and went to sleep, his thoughts on Candra.

2006 Barbara Moon

CHAPTER FOUR

Inside the Tolden castle, King Stephad ranted at his men: "Where did they go? Who were they, you idiots?" None of the men who had come back had an answer.

"Sire, the latest scouts are right now on their way back with news," one of the king's aides dared reply.

"A good thing for all of you!" barked the angry king. "With your lack of news to report, I was ready to send all of you to the fields and have new guards take your places," he shouted again at the guards.

Just then the door opened and an aide hurriedly pushed a disheveled looking scout through to the throne. Kneeling before Stephad's feet, the scout sensed the king's impatience for answers and hastily reported, "Sire, we do not yet know who they are, but we found the place where they left the known territory and entered The Beyond."

"We must follow them!" ordered the King. Looking down in fear, the scout added, "They've had quite a long head start, Sire."

"What's that to me, you Slug!" thundered the king with his next outburst. "I am Stephad, King of Tolden. No one will outrun or outfox me!" Thrusting his fist into the air, he ordered the nearest aide, "Assemble my best guards! We will discover this plot and put an end to it! Now go! We leave at dawn." The scouts and aides scurried quickly from the room, leaving their king alone with his boiling rage.

Dawn of the third day found Stephad and his men quickly progressing through the deep forest just past The Beyond. It was obvious that the party they were tracking walked as best they could to leave no marks, but at times it was impossible to leave no marks as they passed. Picking up these small signs proved easy for Stephad's scouts. Following his scouts, Stephad pushed the men on relentlessly. Hot sun and scarce water began to wear down the Tolden party. Preoccupied and determined to overtake the rebels ahead, the king seemed blinded to the needs of his people. In stark contrast to the rebels he sought, Stephad traveled without the blessings of The One. He wanted no one to tell him what to do and where to go. Confident in his own strength, the king drove forward without caution, his men continued on with him from fear, not respect.

CHAPTER FIVE

Having broken camp before sunrise, the small Unidan band now stood at the foot of the tall mountain that had seemed so very far away only yesterday. It was yet early in the morning, and they discussed what to do next. The mountain, surrounded by brushy meadows, sat majestically alone, wide and tall, yet not too steep. The parchment translation did not give the exact location of the electrokey. In fact it had provided more of a riddle to be solved. The Unidans were not sure what to do. Should they climb the mountain? Or should they first explore the base to see if their search would give them more clues as to which way to go? And just where was the Dome? It was not clear from the Elders' translation which direction it lay from this spot. Chregg turned to his group, "Let's stop here at the foot of the mountain, consult the translation and talk with The One again. He has promised to give us what we need when it is needed. We are at a place where we need to move carefully and intelligently."

Taking the opportunity to rest, the group sank to the ground in a circle, thankful for time to eat a small bite and drink some water. Brinid withdrew the translation from her pack. She spread it out on the ground and found the riddle the Elder's had deciphered:

> *Deep in the green*
> *Below the blue*
> *Hidden is the key*
> *That opens the true.*
> *Time blooms in the green*
> *And shows it through*
> *Now it is red*
> *Instead of blue.*
> *If time has not come*
> *On one, one has to wait*
> *Only the key*
> *Will open the gate.*

Each of the travelers had read and studied the riddle and wondered about its meaning. Now everyone reread it. Everyone was so excited they began talking at the same time about their ideas. After a few minutes, Eric quieted everyone with a friendly shout, "Hey! One at a time, please."

Candra threw in quickly, "I think we couldn't know until we arrived here at the mountain."

Brinid added, "And I think we have to climb to find our next step or else wouldn't we have been told to just go around it?"

"I am with Brinid on that," Nathan said, nodding his head firmly. "What do you say, Chregg?"

"I think we should first consult The One together and then proceed as He directs. There are yet too many unknowns," replied their leader. Everyone bowed together before their only King. Marland spoke aloud for them, "Oh, One Within. We come humbly before You, united as one with each other and You. We declare that we can do nothing without You, without your help and guidance. You have brought us to this place for the good of Atron. We await Your voice within us all to confirm that we should climb and which direction we should go up. Our thanks to You for revealing all things needed and most of all for Yourself."

Patient and still, the faithful band waited expectantly to hear the words of The One in his or her heart. They knew He would speak and direct, and they would hear His voice. Candra and Eric were the first to look up. They smiled at one another, their bond growing as they looked in each other's eyes and found the love of The One and the certainty of His leading. The others joined them and one by one shared their leadings. Chregg summarized by saying, "We are looking at the West side of the mountain. I am hearing that we should climb and that we should begin on the South side of the face we stand looking at. When we reach that point up there," he said pointing to an area that appeared to be somewhat flat with perhaps a cave behind it, "we shall stop for the night. Is this agreeable to all?"

He looked around the circle seeing nods of agreement from each one and said, "Alright then, let our climb began." Immediately they began to pick their way, following a winding path up the face of the mountain. A little steep, the path proved to be somewhat difficult, but rocks and brush gave hand and footholds to steady their steps as the small group headed toward the large flat area above. The day grew brighter and hotter, and Chregg noticed that his fellow travelers were growing more and weary. "Concentrate, my friends, on our assent," he encouraged, his voice firm and strong. "Each step we take brings us closer and closer to finding the electrokey."

Eric and Nathan had been quietly moving in single file up the rocky trail, when they stopped for a moment to look back at the land they had just come through. This vantage point made other huge creatures like the one they had killed earlier in the day suddenly visible. As one they thought, *so The One protected us more than we knew*. After a moment, Eric asked Nathan, "What might we encounter on our return home? I do not like the looks of those monstrous beasts down there."

"I would not even want to contemplate going back this way if we had to do it alone," Nathan said reassuringly. "I am glad The One is guiding and protecting us."

"Those animals don't all look the same, do they, from here?" Eric continued.

"No, that's true. They're like nothing I'm accustomed to seeing," Nathan huffed as he resumed climbing. "It will be fine with me if we don't get any closer to them than we are right now." Eric nodded as he reached up, searching for the next place to hold as he and Nathan followed the others up the large mountain.

Up ahead the young explorers faintly heard Borg shout encouragingly down the line, "I can see the flat area!" The news quickly spread to the rest of the climbers and one by one they pulled themselves up onto the flat place to rest. Large and open, the travelers saw for the first time that part of the flat area was occupied by a pool of calm blue water measuring about as wide as four men lying end to end. The pool sat at the entrance to a fairly large cave. Flowering bushes edged the cave entrance and part of the pool.

"This is the most beautiful place!" exclaimed Brinid surprised by the cool, serene, but most of all green expanse before her. "What a contrast to the dirty city where I grew up." With the continual presence of water from the pool, each plant was bursting with vibrant color.

"This is not like anything I've seen in the forest," Candra chimed in. "So lovely, I could stay here forever. Can we drink from it and bathe in it, I hope?" From The One, Richen got a sense that the water would be safe. "Come on men, let's venture into the cave to check it out as the women freshen up in the pool," he directed. "And then we can get a fire going."

What a relief for the tired travelers after such a long hot journey! As they waded in at the one shallow end, the women noticed that the bottom of the pool was very, very deeply set into the side of the mountain, making the rim around the deeper water level with the ground. That end of the pool was set right at the entrance to the cave. The water was cool and refreshing, washing away the dirt, grime and thirst that had accumulated over so many days. As the women retreated to the cave to lay out their dripping outer garments to dry, the men took their turn to wash at the shallow end of the pool. After a short time, the men joined the women around the fire leaping brightly outside the cave's mouth. As they ate, they talked about their next move. Soon the sun would move down behind the trees leaving them in shade before nightfall.

While the others talked quietly after the meal, Brinid's mind drifted back to the riddle. As she pondered its meaning, she softly repeated it from memory.

> *Deep in the green*
> *Below the blue*
> *Hidden is the key*
> *That opens the true.*
> *Time blooms in the green*
> *And shows it through*
> *Now it is red*
> *Instead of blue.*
> *If time has not come*
> *On one, one has to wait*
> *Only the key*
> *Will open the gate.*

Others, resting alongside her, thanked The One for the pool that was so welcome and refreshing; and for the protection of a sheltering a cave where they could sleep in peace. Brinid was studying the water when suddenly something caught her eye. She crawled over to its edge to make sure she had really seen it. "Look! Look, Everyone!" Look at the water! Now it is green, below the blue!"

Suddenly Candra appeared at her side, "Oh, my word! Brinid's right!" she shouted. Look!"

Others gathered around the pool. "I can't see it," Nathan wailed. "Where do you see it?"

"Come down here, Nate, near us! Maybe it has something to do with the sunlight and the angle," Candra urged, pulling him down by his trouser leg.

Now lined up with Candra and Brinid, everyone could see how the water that had first been blue was now turning deep green below its surface. "It's a sign from the riddle! This must be where the key is," Eric exclaimed, looking around at everyone as they knelt or stooped, crowding the water's edge.

"Quickly Brinid, say the riddle," Nathan and Eric said at the same time.

"Time blooms in the green, And shows it through, Now it is red, Instead of blue," she quoted from memory as they all rolled the words around in their heads trying to complete the puzzle that would lead them to the electrokey.

"If we couldn't see the green when we first arrived and yet now we can, time must have something to do with the colors changing," speculated Eric eagerly.

"Could that mean that we have to be here at a specific time for some kind of blooming flower to come, too?" speculated Brinid. "Maybe something will turn red if that is the case," she continued thinking aloud. "Could it be that we have to be here in a certain season for that to happen, and we aren't?"

"Yes," Candra added, her thoughts moving quickly. "The rest of the riddle says, 'If the time has not come, On one, one has to wait, Only the key, Will open the gate.'" She questioned out loud, "Could the word 'one' here mean our One? He made the seasons and the exact moment that each plant comes into bloom."

Jaren, who had been kneeling at the water's edge, sat back so she could better talk with the whole group. "I believe the One has brought us here in His timing. Does it not make sense, then, that this is the right season for us to be here? He has guided us to this flat area right here on the side of this mountain. It seems to me that every step has been directed by Him."

"You're right," Candra nodded her head. "Yes, you're right. We can see that the water's green as the sun is setting, let's wait around the pool for whatever else might happen until it is too dark for us to see."

"Quickly, spread yourselves around the deep part of the pool at the level where we were able to see the green," directed Chregg. "We can move a bit up and down to see if the angle at which we see the green changes any as the sun begins to set behind the trees."

Expectantly, the searchers spread out around the pool, every eye firmly fixed on the water. They were so intent that they could almost feel the setting sun glide across the sky. Candra was now thankful for how much patience she had learned as she rested and waited by the pool, watching for signs of change. In the days before finding the parchment, she had been so eager for a journey, any journey – even one that The One had not sanctioned. How glad she now was for parents and others in their camp who had continually reminded her of the importance of waiting on His timing. *How has this happened?* she wondered. *I guess all that practice and waiting have helped to remove some of that pull in me to hurry.* And finally here she was, a first hand witness watching as all the dreams of her people might finally come true. Feeling overwhelmed with joy she waited quietly with the others, glad to have grown, glad to be there. The sun continued to move, and suddenly Candra saw the reflection! "THERE!!" She screamed excitedly. "There! There is a flower! I can see the leaves and the red bloom!"

As the group moved quickly to her side each member let out a small gasp, there it was: the red, blooming in the green and turning the blue water to red with its brilliance. No such flower had ever been seen by any of them. They could not believe their eyes! Only for a brief moment and from that specific angle, could they see the flower. Then the sunlight faded over the pond, right before it passed out of sight below the horizon.

With presence of mind, Richen and Nathan hurriedly ran to mark the spot where they had seen the bloom. The riddle was coming true before their eyes! *This has to have something to do with where the electrokey is hidden,* they thought. There was a small celebration as everyone else jumped up and down, cheered and hugged one another. After allowing the celebration to continue a bit, Chregg raised his hand to quiet the group. "It's time," he began, "for us to thank The One and then decide who will go under the water's surface to find the key. We will rest here until we have the full light of the morning." All knelt in thanks to The One for His help in completing this part of the journey. Joden asked The One to show them who would go down into the water to look for the key. A prompting came to the brother and sister of Unidan that they should go together. One would search behind the plant and bloom while the other kept an eye out for danger. "Nathan," Candra spoke first. "I am honored to be even part of this journey. I have long waited for this day and often we have talked about whether it would ever come. I want you to be the one to search for the key. I want to be at your side to help in any way I can."

"Thank you, My Sister and Companion," Nathan returned. "I will accept your wish. AND," he added exuberantly, "I CAN'T WAIT!"

Cheers and shouts erupted as the others joined in Nathan's exhilaration. The chatter and excitement continued until they bedded down for the night.

Everyone had difficultly falling asleep after such an exciting day of discovery. Their people had been longing for such a day since the Elders could remember. Nathan thought about The One's faithfulness. *You do bring things to pass in Your time,* he began. *My One, I am so grateful that You allowed me to be part of this great event,* he continued. *Thank you. Rest us all for the next part of the journey. You are great and you are our one and only King. Thank you, too, for bringing Brinid and Eric to us. Show me what You want for me concerning Brinid. She warms my heart and being with her these weeks has shown me how wonderful she is. I wait on You, I love you, I think I love her. . ."* the young man said as he drifted off to sleep.

CHAPTER SIX

The following morning everyone woke up rested and eager to see what this new day would bring. The sun beamed again on their side of the mountain, bright and warm, and celebration returned as everyone gathered around the marked place in the pond. One team member had thoughtfully brought a rope and some small rocks to help Nathan and Candra's with their dive. The siblings removed any excess clothing and Candra rebound her long braid, winding it into a knot. As she and Nathan entered the water right where the mark had been drawn, Borg handed Nathan a stick.

They dove together, searching for the red bloom nestled in the green leaves of the unfamiliar underwater plant. This time they did not need the sunlight's angle having marked the spot for the beautiful exotic plant. Nathan saw the flower first. Candra watched as he carefully poked at the plant with his stick. They had seen no evidence of animal life in the water, but since their encounter with the huge creature, everyone in the party had become extra cautious. Nathan and Candra waited for a few seconds, but nothing swam out of the plant and so they looked closer, but neither of them could find any poisonous-looking spines or other signs of danger.

Nathan calmly pushed the leaves aside and Candra pulled a handful back to help him better see the bloom. Probing the plant with his fingers, Nathan found a small niche behind the plant, an indentation among the rocks around the wall of the pond. His fingers continued to explore until they touched a hard smooth object shaped like the handle of a Tazor. At first he pulled gently, and then he tugged more strongly until the object came out of the niche and into his hand, fitting comfortably in his palm. He motioned to Candra that they could now swim to the top, following closely behind her.

Searching the plant for the electrokey had taken almost every bit of air, so as they broke the surface of the water, they gasped, filling their tortured lungs with fresh air. Joden and Richen pulled them out of the water, wrapped blankets around them and then led them to the campfire. Nathan laid the shiny object eagerly on the ground for all to see. Long and smooth, it was made of a bright shiny material different from any they ever had seen. Nathan turned the item around slowly. Along one side there was a slit, surely the way to open the object. Nathan turned to Brinid, "Daughter of the Toldens," he grinned, "Would you like to try and open it?"

Brinid met his grin with a modest smile. "I would be honored, Nate, Son of Unidan. May The One have His way in the reuniting of our two peoples," she added shyly as she took the object, lightly placing the blade of her Sedat into the narrow opening. Gently she worked at prying the object open, *don't hurry too much, or you'll break the blade,* she reminded herself, as the opening slowly grew larger.

"AHHHH!!!" whispered the crowd as she opened the outer shell to reveal another object inside which glowed brightly as the sun struck it for the first time. From all the clues they had followed, they recognized the electrokey, though no one had known exactly what to expect. From its glow, they could tell that it would work something like their Tazors, energized by the sun's rays. Peeking out from under the electrokey, Brinid could see a soft folded piece of material. She turned and passed the electrokey in its holder to Eric. "Your turn, Eric. See what's under the key."

Eric carefully removed the piece of material while the key stayed in its position in the holder. As he unfolded the material, he held it out to his fellow travelers, "There are symbols and lines that seem to form some sort of a drawing." Several onlookers turned and murmured to each other, "What is it?" Marland spoke, "It looks like we've another map." Eric spread the piece of material onto his lap, smoothing it flat. Quietly, everyone studied the drawing, each trying to decipher its meaning.

After some time, Chregg spoke aloud what others were thinking. "I think this must be the mountain we are on," he said pointing to the middle. "And I think that is the Dome behind it, to the right. I'm not sure what to make of the other lines. They look somewhat like what was written on the parchments. What do you young people think?"

Nathan, leaning over Eric's shoulder, pressed forward for a better look. "Yes! I think you're right, Chregg!" he exclaimed. "The old king must have left this. Surely it will save us a lot of time. I'm ready to press on! Let's make a plan!"

"Calm down, Nathan," chided his sister with a laugh. "We still don't know what dangers we might face. Remember that huge beast?"

Eric poked Nathan with his elbow to remind him of the animals they had seen from the heights of the mountain.

"She's right," Eric responded, turning to Nathan. "Do we not always seek The One for our moves?"

"Everyone," said Borg in agreement, "let's do just that." The happy chattering quieted and sitting right where they were, they began talking with The One Within. Talking to Him helped them focus for a moment on all that had already happened and all that lay before them, and thinking about how important finding the Dome would be to the future of their whole world.

"I believe," Borg continued as one by one the Participants raised their heads when finished, "that the next step is to send several scouts to find a way down the north face, heading towards the backside of the mountain. When they find a way down, we will continue our trek eastward, believing that the Dome lies in that direction. Do we agree?"

The members of the group nodded their assent, and those chosen for the scouting team set out with hopes of bringing back news of the new route by next morning. Those who remained rested and talked about the electrokey, which glowed whenever the cover was opened. It was beautiful and mysterious at the same time.

CHAPTER SEVEN

"Sire, we will be in position to catch the rebels by tomorrow morning, according to the returning scouts," King Stephad's most trusted guard reported. "They were spotted on the side of the mountain once the mountain came into view this morning"

"Humph . . . good," growled the weary King. "So . . . we have traveled fast enough." He turned his eyes away, looking toward the mountain, thinking for a few moments. Then he turned back to his aide giving orders, "We will place ourselves so as to be ready for their decent. Whatever these Unidans find, we will take for ourselves," he spat with a wicked chuckle as he thought about the surprise his men had in store for their enemies. "And we'll leave none of them to return to Unidan to tell of it." After a moment, he added brusquely, "Watch out for those beasts. I do not want to lose any more men to them." The guard excused himself from his ill-tempered king, leaving Stephad to stew over this alone. *What can be the reason for this band of rebels to be venturing into the unknown?* the King wondered. *It will be to my benefit to find out, I am certain. Tomorrow will not come too soon.*

The next morning, the King and his few remaining men moved stealthily towards the North side of the mountain looking for places from which they could observe the party of travelers without being noticed. They were keeping careful watch from their hiding places when the band of Unidans, having broken camp earlier, began to wind their way towards the back of the mountain. A returning scout had reported to the Tolden King, "It appears that the party is going to descend the mountain from the back of the North side and then continue their journey." Stephad turned and commanded his men "Move quietly to intercept these intruders. Make sure you remain under cover. We will surprise them when they reach the bottom of the mountain."

# # # #

Nathan, Eric, Candra and Brinid were so excited they could hardly keep from dancing as the four followed the others down the rock trail that wound its way down the back side of the mountain. Tucked within her shirt, Brinid carried the electrokey safely hidden inside a pouch dangling from a rawhide string tied safely around her neck. Recent news from the returning scouts kept everyone thinking. When they reported back, they said, "We have seen what must be the Dome out in the distance! We could see the sunlight reflecting off of something quite large and high!" Candra, still having difficulty containing her happiness, stepped closer to Eric and touched his shoulder as they walked single file down the slope. "Oh, Eric," she whispered, clapping her hands together, "can you believe we are about to see the Dome?"

Eric put his hand behind his back for her to take and turned his head to look at his beloved's glowing face. "Yes, it is hard to believe," he agreed. "And for me even more so since I've known all of you and The One for such a short time."

"I think I understand what you're saying, Eric. But isn't it wonderful that we can know Him so easily when our hearts are turned towards Him? Time means little to Him, and love means everything. He blesses all of us.

We easily forget that He is timeless. We easily forget many things, but His great love brings us back to a right focus when we forget the details."

"Candra," Eric said so softly that she almost didn't hear him. "Have you come to know His other kind of love that we spoke of earlier?"

Candra searched her thoughts for just a moment before answering. Her timid smile seemed rather out of place for such a valiant warrior as she had proved herself to be, but this was new territory, and for her, therefore very important. "I know now that I loved you the first time I watched you awaken in Gran's tent. Such feelings were new to me and almost frightening to feel, especially when they were for a Tolden. But, yes, Eric, I know His other kind of love and it is for you."

At that moment, Eric did not care that they were descending a mountain in a place he knew little about, or that they were sweaty and tired. He simply stopped where he was, turned, and looked up at those dazzling blue eyes that he had first gazed into while so wounded and hurt, and put his hands on Candra's shoulders as she stepped nearer. "I love you very much, Candra, the Beloved One. Will you be my Beloved One as well?" The look in her eyes gave the answer he wanted and he drew her close into his arms.

The sudden quiet behind him, made Nathan turn just in time to see the top of his sister's head over Eric's shoulder. Ever the amiable tease, he stopped the others with his laughing announcement, "Look, Everyone! It seems we have some new future Last Companions!"

Brinid, already stepping carefully towards the couple after overhearing part of their conversation, threw her arms around them both as Nathan's arms met hers around Eric's back. "Whoweeee!" crowed Nathan. "Careful on this trail here. Whoweeee!" The chorus rang out again as the others joined in this latest celebration. Laughing and calling congratulations, they continued their careful descent.

The joyful band of travelers rounded the Eastern face of the mountain as they picked their way down the rocky trail. Soon they were able to see land on the other side. One by one each glimpsed for the first time off in the distance, the long held dream of their people—the lost Dome of Atron. The sun reflected so brilliantly off the roof of the Dome that it was easy to see even at this distance. Once again the observers quietly realized they were beholding yet another beautiful and unexplainable mystery, much like the electrokey and the underwater plant. There was something mysterious about each one, something not of their world. What more wondrous things would this journey have for them?

"Friends!" Chregg announced with delight, "as soon as we arrive at the bottom we will decide how much further to walk this day. Perhaps it will only take one full day to make it to the Dome." The party, unaware that more than a campsite would await them as they reached the bottom, continued its slow descent down the side of the mountain.

CHAPTER EIGHT

Stephad and his men rounded the side of the mountain catching sight of a bright reflection in the distance. From the angle they had taken to round the mountain, they were too low to see the Dome itself. Nobody could figure out what was causing the brightness, including the King himself. *Could it have something to do with this bunch of rebels and the purpose for their journey?* He kept pushing back the rumors, rumors that had always floated around Tolden, now niggling at the back of his mind and instead focused on his overwhelming need to destroy these people and the rest of Unidan.

Stephad, the self-assured King of Tolden, directed his men to their places behind several large bushes that grew near the base of the mountain. They quietly lay in readiness for their surprise ambush of the Unidans now descending the mountain. *I will let them live just long enough to force them to tell me of their plans.* The arrogant king was unaware that two Unidan scouts had remained behind at the bottom while the rest had returned to direct the remaining travelers around and down the mountain. From their hidden positions the scouts had picked up the Toldens' movements, and one of the scouts quietly moved back up the mountain to warn the rest of the group.

As word of the menacing Toldens quietly moved up the trail, the Unidans appeared on the outside as if they were totally unaware of the Toldens' presence while inside they prepared their hearts before The One. Those armed with Tazors casually dangled their hands at their sides while the others carefully drew their Sedats and hid them in their shirtsleeves. As the last Unidan stepped onto the plain scattered with rocks, brush and large bushes, the Tolden attackers rushed out from their hiding places and ran towards the Unidans with weapons drawn.

Before the Toldens could fire, Unidan Tazors blasted a fierce light of extra power into their midst causing the Tolden attackers to drop as one to the ground. Stephad, who had been running through the midst of his soldiers, stumbled and almost dropped his Tazor, as his eyes locked with those of another Tolden. His brother Eric was standing ready with Tazor pointed, near one of the large bushes. Recovering his footing and his composure, Stephad strutted toward his brother, the Second Prince of Tolden. "It cannot be you!" he bellowed. "You are supposed to be dead and out of my life!" "AND!" his screams continued to pierce the air, "Why are you dressed like a Unidan?"

Eric readied his Tazor, awaiting his brother's strike. "I am not just dressed like a Unidan, Brother," he answered firmly and without fear, "I *am* a Unidan!" In that split second, Eric was not certain what he should do next. He did not want to kill his brother, even in self-defense. He continued to think, his eyes continuing to study those of his evil brother and the Tazor in his hand. Suddenly, his brother's face changed from rage to terror. Following his brother's gaze, Eric saw what had frozen his brother with horror. Before Eric could make a move, something large and fragrant sped past the top of his head and swooped down over Stephad, covering him completely. In an instant, the gigantic flower had snatched Stephad up and swallowed him like an insect, and then disappeared immediately into the midst of the large bush behind Eric.

Dazed but alert Eric tried to refocus on the battle all around him. Things were already quieting, with but a few Toldens remaining on their feet. With Stephad gone, those who remained began laying their weapons on the ground. Stephad was not the only Tolden to fall prey to the gigantic bush flowers, but miraculously the flowers had only attacked Toldens in their feeding frenzy. During the commotion of the flower attacks, the Unidans had routed the rest of the Toldens using their superior Tazor fire. As silence settled over the plain, the Unidans quietly surrounded the remaining Toldens and tied them together until a decision could be made as to what to do with them. Four members of the Unidan band had been slightly wounded. Eric sank to his knees, completely exhausted in body and mind. Candra ran to his side.

"Who was that in front of you?" she questioned earnestly. She knelt and put her hand on his shoulder. "You paused instead of firing!"

Eric started weeping. His heart felt soft and full of pain. He sat with his beloved's arm pulled tightly around him as he sobbed deeply over the loss of his brother. As they knelt there, a feeling of forgiveness spread inside and settled alongside the pain in his heart. *I never thought I would feel this way towards Stephad,* he thought to himself. *I did not know I could love someone who was so hateful and cruel to me for so long. It must be The One.* After a few minutes, Eric sighed and wiped his eyes on his sleeve. He looked up at Candra, Nathan and Brinid joining her at his side. The women bound up the wounded while Marland and Chregg kept an eye on the remaining Toldens. "That was the new King of Tolden," Eric whispered as a shudder ran through his body. "He was my brother, my twin. His attire tells me that my Father is also dead. Stephad wore the armor of the king."

"What a horrible thing to see," comforted Candra with tears in her eyes. "Those flowers were gigantic, like the creature we killed earlier. A few of the other Toldens were also taken by the flowers, but to watch that happen to someone you knew—I don't think there are any words to help."

"I feel so sad for you, Eric. May The One comfort and heal you with His truth," added Nathan. With tears in her eyes, Brinid just gave Eric a hug. For a few moments, the friends sat there, silently embracing one another.

Chregg waited until the first shocks of the ambush lessened, then gathered the group together. They did not know when or if the bush flowers would decide to eat again. Some thought that perhaps The One had used the huge flowers to help them win against the Toldens, but nobody wanted to stay around to find out. After conferring, they decided to send the remaining Toldens back to the known territory, along with two wounded Unidans, two Unidan fighting men and Eric. As much as it disappointed him not to be able to go into the Dome this first time, Eric knew that as the only heir to the throne of Tolden he was now the King. He would have to return to Tolden, and with the guidance of The One, begin the work of making changes in the city. The others would find him there upon their return.

Calling Candra aside, Eric lovingly took both her hands and looked deeply into her beautiful blue eyes. "I will miss you so. I have to go back, but I want you to go on to the Dome. I will speak to The One on your behalf and for your safety."

Candra let go of his hands and grabbed his neck, crying as she had never cried before. "I love you, Eric, King of Tolden. I feel so torn between two great desires," she sobbed as Eric held her closely for a moment. Candra held tightly to his neck, until her sobs began to slow. At last she sighed peacefully. "But I know deep inside I am to continue to the Dome. How I will miss you!" she said.

The new King drew back his face and tipped hers up so he could look into the eyes of his future Companion. Even within his own pain of losing his family, Eric had great hope. Wiping away his own tears with one arm, he smiled and looked at his future standing before him and asked with a grin,

"Is it permitted in Unidan for future Last Companions to share a kiss before their ceremony?"

She quickly answered with a smile of her own, "Only if others are present and the two are agreed!"

They were--and so they did. The rest of the party cheered and thanked The One for this very tangible sign of the future reuniting of Atron. Finally the two parties split, going their separate directions, as Nathan, Brinid, Candra, Chregg and the remaining Participants headed East towards the shining Dome.

Part Three: Inside the Dome

CHAPTER ONE

It was with mixed emotions that the nine Unidans left Eric and the company returning with him, to finish their adventure. Journeying eastward, they again found themselves in a forest that lay between them and the long sought after entrance to the Dome. In the brilliant afternoon sun, the Dome's roof reflected a variety of colors into the air above the top of the Dome. The rainbow of colors could be seen now and then through the canopy of trees as the travelers wove their way through the forest. Assuming there were no more big problems, Chregg estimated that the travelers would perhaps only have to camp one more night before reaching the outer wall of the Dome. Though weary from the strain of battle, both with the Toldens and the unexpected creatures living in this part of Atron, everyone felt exhilarated and strangely energized as they were moving closer and closer to the answers that the Dome would hold for their people.

Candra's thoughts were a jumbled mess bouncing back and forth between the Dome and Eric. *What a time to be alive!* she thought gladly in her heart. *What a wonderful person The One has brought to me, to all of us even. I am going to see the unification of Atron become a reality. I can't wait to see Father, Mother, Gran, all our people again and tell them of our adventures.* Candra's ponderings had so slowed her steps that, hurrying to catch up, she called to her brother who was walking ahead with Brinid, "Hey, Nathan!" she shouted. "Wait for me. I'm so full of joy that it's hard to keep myself from dancing. If I weren't so tired, I just might dance through these woods."

The two who were up ahead slowed and adjusted their pace as Candra caught up with them. "This electrokey hanging around my neck keeps reminding me that we are really here and it's not just a dream," said Brinid as she drew the case from her shirt and looked at it for the hundredth time.

"And being able to see the Dome's roof through the tree tops when we hit a clearing reminds me," added Nathan. "How big do you suppose it is, Girls?"

"It seems to grow bigger the closer we get, doesn't it?" Brinid said with a smile. "It won't be long until we can actually touch its walls and look at it for ourselves."

"Yes," answered Candra, grabbing both their hands and pulling them along to quicken the pace. "Let's walk faster. I cannot wait!"

Soon all nine were picking up the pace, wanting to reach the side of the Dome as quickly as they could manage. The trees had become thicker again, hiding the Dome from view. Suddenly, Borg, the lead scout, was lifted from the forest floor, disappearing into thick branches in the trees. His yelp of surprise was quickly muffled and from where they were standing, the other eight were unable to locate him. Remembering their training, the Participants formed a circle with their backs to one another, weapons drawn, waiting while Chregg quickly assessed the situation to give further directions. "Joden and Richen," he said pointing to the two Participants," check out the trees over where Borg disappeared while the rest of us cover you."

The two stepped under the huge branches of the trees and looked up, searching for any signs of their comrade. Joden saw him first. "There!" she said, pointing up at a large branch a few feet away. "There he is, Richen." It was not a good sight. A large vine, wound around his body, was trying to choke the life from Borg. This was not like any vine the Unidans had ever seen in their part of Atron. It was mysteriously flexible to be so large. Yelling for the others, Richen and Joden ran towards the tree with their Tazors drawn. "Oh, One," Richen began to pray as they ran, "I ask that you protect our friend from this hideous vine. Show us what to do to help save him. Only You can help us." The others quickly joined them, surrounding the tree as Richen and Joden searched for the end of the vine. "I found it, right here," Joden yelled, pointing to a place among the bushes that surrounded the large tree. The flexible vine was part of the roots protruding from the bottom of the tree. It traveled upwards into the branches, clinging as it went until it disappeared into the thick foliage overhead.

"Can you see if Borg is still breathing?" Richen asked the others as he studied the vine more closely. "I need to be certain he won't get hurt worse if we slash the vine here at the root."

Marland answered quickly, "I can see him breathing, but the vine is almost covering his face. I think its best that we hurry. Consulting The One, she directed, "Cut the vine, Richen, and everyone else get ready to catch Borg as he falls. Watch out for backlashes from the vine when it's cut because it can manipulate its entire length."

"Everyone ready?" Chregg asked as he swiftly removed his cloak and spread it out for others to grab a hold of. "Go, Richen. Cut it!" Chregg said as the others grabbed a section of the cloak and steadied themselves under

Borg's wrapped up body. Whispers to The One could be heard all around the perimeter of the heavy cloak.

With a swift hack to the thick vine, Richen's Tazor sliced it clean through. There was an audible screech as the vine throbbed and thrashed all along the tree trunk. As soon as the thrashing reached the top of the vine, its end began to unravel and Borg fell, landing perfectly in the middle of Chregg's cloak. Chregg and Jored slung the edges of the cloak over Borg and ran with him back to the edge of the trees. The others drew Tazors and Sedats as the vine continued to thrash its way down the tree. As it fell, the thrashing made it appear that it was still alive and the Participants were prepared to fire. When the top of the vine hit the forest floor, it slithered so quickly towards Jored's feet that she was unable to get away. The others could see how the vine had captured Borg, but that would not happen this time. Four bright blasts of energy hit the twisting vine at the same time and it finally lay still. "Thank You, One," puffed six relieved voices in unison. "Now lets see how Borg is," said Marland as they all turned to go back to the edge of the trees.

Borg was lying on the ground while Chregg and Jored were looking over his wounds. The vine had secreted some kind of liquid on to Borg, but it had not penetrated his clothing. He had some whelps on his arms, legs and face, but the quick rescue by his friends had kept his injuries to the minimal.

"My friends, how grateful I am to you and The One that I am alive." The others bent to lay their hands on Borg and help him to sit up. "I never want to go through that again," Borg said. "What is it with the plants and animals out here? Do you think The One will show us?"

"In His time, perhaps," answered Chregg. "Now do you think you can walk?"

"I think so. Let me try." Two of the men helped Borg to his feet and helped him take a few steps. "It seems that all is well," he said as he tottered a few paces then steadied himself on Jored's shoulder. "Maybe a stick will help steady me for a while," he chuckled as he walked around looking like one of the elders. "It's not every day that a man gets jerked into a tree and with the hopes of being made into a meal." Sounds of laughter signaled the relief each Participant felt as each one picked up their supplies and readied to move out. As they continued moving toward the Dome, Chregg instructed everyone, "Stay close together and keep watch all around you as you walk. Weapons set to ready. We knew this might get dangerous. We couldn't have known the dangers would be such large and strange ones. Yet The One is with us no matter what happens, so remember this: He is our courage. Let's move on."

A little subdued, the Participants quietly discussed what happened with Borg and the giant vine. Coming face to face with these strange plants and animals and their feeding habits was very frightening and had tempered their excitement about the Dome for the moment. *What makes the forest so different here?* Many were thinking.

Nathan, talking under his breath to The One as he walked, asked for protection and then thanked Him for the many times He had obviously already taken care of them. He motioned for Brinid and Candra to walk in front of him. Sobered by the events of the past few moments, other party members worked to adjust their focus, approaching the mission with a heightened sense of awareness of what might be just ahead of them.

Cautiously, they moved forward without further attacks and soon found they were close enough to see the Southwest side of the Dome. Their first real glimpses, revealed a large round building, with an apex so high that it towered far above them -- as much as fifteen men standing on each other's shoulders. "Oh, Wow!" Nathan exclaimed, as others stood silently around him, awed by the great structure. "There must be more treasures in there than we could ever imagine. I think it will take us a long time to see all that's there."

"That's for sure, Nate," Brinid agreed reverently. "Its size reminds me somewhat of the Tolden city," she added. "While it took me a little time to walk around the perimeter of that city, exploring what was on the inside took much longer." The group remained quiet and still, each savoring this long anticipated moment, until Brinid broke their reverie by pointing towards the roof of the Dome, and adding with great enthusiasm, "How beautiful! The material the Dome is made from is unlike anything we have seen in either place-- Unidan or Tolden."

As the dwindling sunlight struck the material that made up the top of the Dome, colors of every hue shot back into the sky around the Dome, bursting forth as if in a dance. While Candra watched her heart sang with the dance. *I have never seen anything so marvelous in my life and the closer we get, the more beautiful it seems to grow.*

"Let's stop here and thank The One for all He has done these days to get us to this point – so near the Dome," Chregg said as he motioned for the others to sit. "We will seek His wisdom for what to do next—where and how do we find the exact spot to use the electrokey? Should we sleep before entering?"

After some moments of quiet reflection and listening, Nathan broke the silence. "It seems to me that we should rest here and then continue to walk towards the South side, then begin circling around the Western side until we complete the circle. As we make a loop around the Dome, we need to keep our eyes alert and sharply focused in case more unusual creatures decide to surprise us while we look for some kind of door and a slot into which the electrokey might fit." The others agreed.

Chregg finished giving directions from The One. "If we don't find a door before dark, we will stop the search wherever we are, and camp there until morning, continuing our search at dawn. If we find the door, we'll wait until morning to enter. It seems best to have a fresh start when we go inside. If no one else has any input, let's go."

CHAPTER TWO

Now almost back to the city, Eric thoughts during the long trek home had centered on asking The One how he could best help his people. In his heart, he already knew there would have to be tremendous changes and that those changes would take time. Though new at this, he also sensed that his leadership would be effective only by knowing and hearing The One's instructions. The city and its people, long neglected by his father and those who ruled before him, had many needs that would have to be addressed. Nothing that Eric had inherited was organized, except the guards. Everything that had already been in place had been set up to serve only the latest kings' desires for power. Unidans were being used as slave workers in the fields. Children ran wild in the streets without training or schooling, and some without even a place to call home. And as far as he knew, no one who called himself a Tolden knew the Truth from the Ancients or about The One. The task before him seemed daunting. *I hope there are some who remember my mother and her sister*, he thought, recounting Brinid's story in his head. *If I thought I had this to do alone, I would really feel overwhelmed. But I'm not alone and will never be again,* his heart rejoiced. *I have The One, my future Companion, and the other Unidan people to help me. The One will bring to pass what He has declared,* he found himself thinking as his little group traveled back toward civilization.

# # # #

At the very same moment that Eric was pondering his next steps towards freedom and unity for his people, the travelers he had left behind cheered with such gusto it was a wonder Eric had not heard them. After following their plan to continue walking south, the anxious explorers had finally reached their destination: the wall of the Dome.

Each person touched the wall, almost reverently, hardly believing that they were finally there. The wall was made of a material unfamiliar to the travelers. Shiny like the Dome, it had a texture to it, while the Dome itself seemed like it would be smooth to the touch. Richen drove a stick into the ground to mark the spot as their starting place so that they would know when they had completed a circle around the Dome. Staying fairly close to the huge wall, the group began walking again, following the Westerly curve of the wall, inspecting it for any changes that might resemble a door.

In a short while, the travelers at the back of the line could hear another cheer. It was Nathan. Everyone broke into a run to see Nathan pointing towards an indention: "It looks like a door of sorts! See!" he said, his finger tracing an invisible line in the air, "All the way around to this spot the pattern of the wall has looked the same, but these lines look different. This has to be it!" He moved closer and began moving his hands in a pattern that mirrored a seam that formed the shape of a very large door. The rest of the wall for as far as they could see, had horizontal lines etched into it. If this were indeed a door, it would be by far the largest one any of them had ever seen. A man balancing on another's shoulders could walk through it without bending his head to go through the opening. And it was as wide as five people standing with arms outstretched, hand to hand.

As everyone stood in awe of the real possibility of entering the great Dome, the sun slid lower and lower behind the trees surrounding the Dome. Chregg broke the silence. "We will wait until morning to try the electrokey in the door. Let's make our camp right here near the wall and try to rest for a while so that we'll be ready to enter the Dome at first light."

Marland began to gather wood to make a fire while Joden and Richen hunted for food. Jaren, following an almost dried up stream, came to a small indentation where she found a little water, which she collected for the thirsty travelers. Everyone, wanting to stay busy, worked hard at their assigned tasks and yet found their thoughts wandering again and again to the Dome and what they might find inside. Soon the camp was made, food had been eaten, and everyone settled down by the light of the campfire as darkness came. As sleep came, their eyes were drawn to the reflection of their fire as it danced along the side of the Dome. Soon, weariness outweighed their anxious feelings about the next day, and only those taking the first shift to guard were left awake. By the time the teams of guards rotated twice, it would be the dawn of a new and very exciting day.

# # # #

As Candra awoke the next morning, the sun was just peeking over the trees, making a beautiful array of colors bounce off the Dome. She poked Brinid in the side urging, "Wake up, sleepy eyes! The sun is shining and today is the day of all days!"

Suddenly roused from a fitful sleep, Brinid stretched her arms and legs, and began to quickly recall the events of the previous day. *Finally, we are at the Dome's door.* She threw off her cloak that had served as an extra cover during the cool night and rose to her knees letting out a yell that echoed the excitement in Candra's voice, "As Nathan says so often, 'Whooee!' Yes! I am ready!"

Thanks to Brinid's whoop of sheer joy, the others awoke, jumped up and began moving about. Briskly putting together a refreshing breakfast, they took time to seek The One's direction for the day within the mysterious Dome. Soon the little band assembled in front of the large door, quietly anticipating what might lie beyond. From inside her shirt, Brinid drew out the soft leather pouch that dangled at the end of a string of hide, tied around her neck. Feeling inside the pouch, her fingers grasped the smooth case, which held the special key. She opened the cover, and just as it had at the pool, the key began to glow. Everyone's eyes turned in amazement and joy, as there on the right side of the door a small rectangle also began to glow. "Look at that!" Nathan exclaimed, "On the door. It's must be the lock! Whooeee!"

Calmly laying her hand on her brother's arm, Candra chuckled, "Slow down, Little Brother. We're going in sooner or later, you know. We have to be careful. We don't want any more surprises, do we, Chregg?" she asked, turning to their wise leader.

"I myself am full of Nathan's enthusiasm," responded Chregg, his smile as big as theirs. "But, yes, we must remember to proceed carefully. Any ideas as to how the key may fit?"

"Why don't we just lay the electrokey onto that rectangle first," offered Brinid as she turned the key over and over in her hand. "See where that glowing spot by the door seems to match this?" She held the electrokey up to the other glowing spot on the door without touching it. It looked like a perfect fit except that the part that was glowing on the door, while it had the same shape, was a bit larger than the key.

"Are we ready then?" asked Nathan again, trying to contain himself as best he could.

"Go ahead, Brinid. Let the key touch the door. Line it up in the center, matching the shapes," said Chregg as the others held their breath in anticipation.

Brinid leaned closer to the door and turned the key in her fingers to align it with the glow on the door, and a blue spark jumped from the door to the key. Brinid leapt back, surprised but unhurt, and then looked at Chregg for further instructions. "What shall I do?" she asked.

"It seems that's part of the operation and it doesn't seem to be harmful. Do you want to try it again or have someone else try? What do you think?"

"I will try again," Brinid answered strongly. "I've felt so honored to be the one to carry the key." This time as Brinid's hand holding the key turned it long ways to line up with the lock, she quickly touched the key to the glowing spot on the door. Instantly, the key moved from her hand and clung to the door, perfectly aligned inside the glowing recessed compartment in the door. In the next moment, the travelers heard a loud, grinding noise. Startled, everyone immediately moved back a few paces from the door. As they watched, slowly but surely, the door began sliding open to their left.

A blast of stale air from inside struck the adventurers in the face. Though no one had been inside the Dome for more time than even Gran knew, the air inside still seemed quite breathable. The group heard a soft sound as the panel slowly slid to a stop on the other side of the doorway. Awed, the travelers stood stunned and silent as the Dome lit up inside as if it were midday instead of early morning. Here was a new puzzle—light that was not from the sky or a fire. What else would they find inside this place that already challenged their minds with such mysteries?

As they hesitantly peeked inside, they saw the beautiful colors reflecting through the top of the Dome to the outside, the ones they had followed the day before. It was so marvelous that they all—even Nathan--remained speechless for a few moments, standing silently inside this grand entrance to the Dome. Many things were unfamiliar to them as they looked around the inside of the Dome. Several sections contained large objects made of materials similar to the electrokey and the top of the Dome. Other sections contained shelves and shelves of books. *Perhaps those hold the ancient books we seek*, thought Candra. Across the room from where they stood were tables set up to do experiments, lined with bottles of various colored liquids and odd-looking instruments. And this was just what they could see from the doorway. Nathan broke the silence. "Oh, wow. Where do we start?"

Cautiously, Candra and Brinid took a step inside. *Where do we begin our search? Look for a way to bring rain? Or find Your books that will help bring peace to Atron?* Candra whispered a prayer to The One. After a few moments, she sensed His direction, and taking Brinid's hand, she took a few slow steps around the right side of the door. There, she found what looked like a small enclosure. Against and out from the Dome walls were sturdy wooden shelves held in place by beautiful white and gray stones. The shelves were lined with many large books. Scattered around in front of the beautiful shelves were several comfortable chairs facing tables, upon which rested covered boxes. In the center stood a dark cabinet upon which rested a large open book.

It was obvious to Candra that the open book held an honored spot among the other beautiful volumes that filled this area of the Dome. She motioned, and the others followed, as she and Brinid stepped up to the cabinet to look more closely at the book. The right side of the book held words, but on the left there was a drawing that immediately caught Candra's attention. It was an exact duplicate of the very parchment that had led them to the Dome. "Oh!" exclaimed Candra and Brinid at the same time. Candra pointed, "Look everyone! A copy of our parchment!"

Chregg and Nathan leaned over the girls' shoulders to see the page and at once recognized the strange writings from the parchment that their Elders had so carefully deciphered. Before their eyes could move to the other page, Candra, jumping up and down with joy, exclaimed, "I can read this! I can read it. Our language hasn't changed in all these years!" Almost knocking the girls over as he moved to get a better look, Nathan began to read aloud:

"This is the last log report before I close the Dome and hide the electrokey that opens it. I do not know how many years will have passed before the Dome opens again. Should you be reading this, it means that you have kept the Parchment safe and you were able to return to the Dome. In this book of reports and the others on the shelves behind it, you will find all that you will need to rediscover the wonders of our Ancients: how we came to Atron, how to keep the planet of Atron healthy, experiments that we carried out to help our people, and still many other works we participated in and facts and truths we have learned since being here. Some of the reports will tell you where to look for explanations or how to find instructions you need. We have used both the ancient means of handwriting and, most recently, recording devices that have been invented in the years since the Ancients have been gone. All of this has been preserved for you so that you might explore and learn the ways of the ones who brought us here to Atron.

Signed,
Damond
Son of Vandlyn
Son of Atron and the One"

"What are recording devices?" Brinid wondered aloud, looking to the others one by one for an answer.

"It feels like I don't know anything anymore," answered Borg for all of them. "Large creatures, huge meat eating flowers and vines, materials we have never seen or touched, lights from nowhere--I need a little time to sit down and think within."

The Participants sat down, making a circle around the large cabinet, and closed their eyes to listen within. After a moment, Candra spoke aloud to The One, " O Marvelous One, we come with deep thankfulness to You that we have arrived safely here at the lost Dome. We thank You for allowing us to be part of Your plan that will save our world. But we don't know where to start; it all seems so overwhelming."

Nathan continued, "What would You have us do first? Where do we start? Can we really help the rain come again?"

Brinid was the next one to speak from her heart. "We cannot thank You enough, One, for being in us and directing us. We wait for Your leading with assurance and hope, willing to do as You say."

As Brinid finished, Chregg stirred and the others looked up with understanding in their eyes. Chregg put the plan of The One into words. "It seems to me that we are to first explore inside without touching anything. But we need to find out how to keep the light coming in so that we can close the door. After we look around more closely, we will then decide how we should continue. Marland can read the log report book for a bit of history, skipping around in it as needed. Do we agree that our first big task is to find out how to make the rains come again?"

Nodding, the others quickly stood up, ready to explore. *Nothing is impossible with the One*, Candra reminded herself as His peace flowed through her body. Thankful for His presence, she continued, *how would we be able to move without His love and hope?* She turned to the large shelves of books behind the cabinet and began to read some of their titles. "Look, Everyone! Maybe these will help," she pointed. They all gathered around the books and Chregg ran a careful finger down some of the titles.

"*EXPERIMENTS*," he read. Moving to another he continued, "*RECORDING DEVICES*" and here is the one that Gran will love," chuckled Chregg as his fingers traced the title, *"MEDICINE."* "And here is one that says, *'EARLY HISTORY,'*" he said, moving his fingers softly along another spine. "Here it is . . . the one we need first—*'OPERATION OF THE DOME!'* And next to it," he added with a cheer, *"'WEATHER HEALTH!'"*

Instantly a cheer went up from the small group of Participants. They had found the help they needed. Chregg directed Nathan and Eric to check the book marked "Operation" first to find out how to close the door and yet keep the light. They accomplished this quickly as they found the place in the book that told them about "buttons in the wall" that they could push and where to find them. "Now we will be able to break up into teams to explore throughout the Dome. We will need to be careful not to disturb anything that's yet unfamiliar," their leader directed. "For the rest of today, let's stay together and wait until tomorrow to read the section on 'Weather'." Reaching agreement, the group began to explore what lay to the right of the beautiful case that held the log report and the other books. Later, Chregg said, "We will need to make sure we have enough food and water for tomorrow. Joden and Richen, will you go out hunting and then bring it back into us here? Jored, could you find more water?"

CHAPTER THREE

After firmly establishing his right to the throne upon his return, one of the first tasks Eric undertook was to free the Unidans who had been working as slaves in the fields. Gathering his high officials together, he issued this decree: "All Unidans are free to come out from hiding and join us here, or go back home to Unidan. Make this known throughout all of Tolden." What a surprise and relief for the vendors in the marketplace and others who had helped supply the people of Unidan with needed wares and information! In order to protect the freed Unidans, Eric also instituted a penalty of death for anyone from Tolden who was convicted of harming someone from Unidan. He rounded up most of Stephad's remaining guards and loyal followers and put them in a dungeon along with the ones that returned from the journey with him. He would deal with them later.

Though he had been concerned about the impact of these drastic changes, Eric soon discovered courtiers and nobles who had secretly shared his mother's and Brinid's parents' dreams and longings. Gaining courage as they listened to Eric tell his story and finding real change as they looked in his eyes, this remnant stepped forward to lend their help and influence. No longer pretending to go along with the plans of the cruel King Krall, they participated in several meetings along with some of the advisors and aides that Eric had inherited from his father and brother. During these meetings, Eric shared what he had learned during his time with the Unidan people, and was able to convince the majority that it would be far better for everyone if the city and the camp worked side by side instead of scheming and warring as enemies.

During the time that Eric awaited the return of his friends from the Dome, he would be busy listening to this newly forged leadership of Tolden and together they would work diligently to improve the plight of their people and move them towards peace with the Unidans. Much of Eric's work was going to involve trips back to Unidan to talk with the Elders and leaders there. Busy though he was, every moment he could spare was spent thinking and wondering about his friends at the Dome. *Are they safe? What have they found? Will the rains come?* Remembering what Handen, Gran and others had encouraged, Eric took those thoughts to The One. Now he would trust and wait as he worked to prepare the city for the Dome travelers' return.

CHAPTER FOUR

At the Dome the travelers had already begun to look more closely at many unfamiliarly shaped items, trying to discover their purposes. At regular intervals, they had discovered stations that had been set up and meticulously stocked for research into further uses of Atron's natural resources. Early in their search, as they followed a sharp curve around the Dome's second corner, everyone recognized sections of living quarters along the outer wall. Sleeping quarters resembled those of the city nobles in Tolden, tables and chairs served as places for eating together or where one could sit comfortably. Having lived under such primitive conditions in their camp, these quarters appeared heavenly to the Unidans and also to Brinid who had spent so much of her life sleeping in the streets.

At first glance it appeared that one section of the living quarters could house about eight individuals and that there were enough sections to accommodate up to fifteen groups of eight. The sections appeared to have been built similarly. After checking things out a little more closely, Chregg directed, "I think this area can be explored more thoroughly without any fear of danger. Let's split into pairs." He motioned each twosome towards a different section to explore. Cries of delight carried above the section walls and into the space above as each pair discovered marvel after marvel. "They've put something together here that somehow makes food just by pushing buttons!" cried Nathan. "And, it also gives water!" he bellowed, laughing as the button he pushed squirted Borg right in the face. "And everything appears to be in working order, I might add," laughed a startled Borg.

"There's a place here in the wall where we can clean our clothes without them getting wet!" the girls squealed.

"We will be able to talk to each other from other places in the Dome by way of this device!" shouted Joden and Richen from their section. "I think we can even see each other while we talk!" Joden exclaimed as she pushed another button.

"I've found out how to control the lights and temperature within each section," Marland added as she blinked the lights off and on. "I think I found something that will allow us to bathe without a creek or river," said Jaren as she turned some knobs and marveled at the warm water coming from some sort of hole in the wall.

"Let's save some of our adventure for tomorrow," teased Chregg. "Come back to the first cubicle. What a place this is!" The four teams quickly gathered and began to share each of their fabulous discoveries, demonstrating for each other how things worked until each one understood the basics. After a few minutes, their leader began calming the group with his voice, "I know we will find other things that will help us, but these seem to be ones we need to know about now. It grows late." The colors glowing outside the Dome diminished as the sun was setting. "Let's remain here for tonight and continue our exploring tomorrow after we check the weather book to see what we need to know to bring rain to our planet. Men, let's sleep here. Marland, you and the other women are free to choose another cubicle down the way." As the group divided and began to disperse, Candra said aloud, "We thank You, One, for these marvelous gifts that will feed and rest us this evening."

CHAPTER FIVE

The Dome radiated vibrant colors from the morning sun as the now refreshed travelers woke and prepared to eat. Breakfast was an experiment in wonder. Utterly fascinated by the new tastes and textures, yet not wanting to waste a thing, the adventurers carefully shared their selections from the food dispensers with each other. Warm water for bathing provided a delightful experience as everyone lathered lavish amounts of the delicious smelling soap that they poured from a cup on the wall. The women especially enjoyed seeing themselves in a reflecting glass that showed their countenances so clearly. With so much pampering, each one's braid was extra neat and slick this morning. After the much-needed rest and refreshment period, smiling faces were everywhere.

Soon Chregg called them together as a group for time with The One. When they had finished singing and talking to The One, Chregg said quietly, "My friends and family, it is time. Only our Elders really know how long all of Unidan has waited for this very day. I wish that all of them could be here with us as we explore and discover these things that, until now, we had only heard were possible. I wish Eric and the others that returned with him were still with us." He looked each one in the eyes and continued, "We are most honored and blessed." Thinking about their adventures so far, Chregg encouraged the group, "The One is within and without and He has the Tempter on a short rope. Let us begin this fresh new morning by continuing to walk the circle in the same direction until we again reach the case that holds the report books. Then, starting with the log report, we will look more closely at the books that we hope will help us find a way to bring rain to our Atron."

As the group continued to circle the inside of the Dome, they soon walked past a spot that looked like it was designed for binding or repairing books. Next they saw an area that had been set up for recycling trash, another for making clothing and of course a section fitted with controls that kept the Dome running. This much was becoming clear: whoever had made this Dome knew mysteries beyond these travelers' imaginations. From what they could see, the Dome seemed to be completely self-sufficient. Everything about it seemed fresh and new – and they knew it had been quite awhile since it had been closed and locked. Their excitement grew with each discovery, with learning more and more about the Dome and the people who had lived there. At last they were coming close to the great door again. Right before they reached it, they saw another large case made of the white and gray stones also lined with wooden shelves. The stones were the same as the ones holding the books they had first encountered and were now headed toward.

Everyone paused in front of the large stone and wood shelves. Like the other one, the case was beautiful. They could see it also held something that looked like books, but these seemed different. "What do you make of these,

Brinid?" asked Nathan, "These books don't look like the others. They're not bound with leather."

"You know, Nathan, on the outside these resemble the case for the electrokey." Turning to Chregg, she asked, "Chregg, would it be alright for us to touch one of these?"

"Yes, go ahead. We have to begin somewhere." Brinid touched one of the strange books with her fingers. It was made of that same hard substance that held the key. Chregg continued, "Go ahead and take it down."

Using two hands, Brinid gently pulled the book from its resting place and held it in her hands. "Nate, you open it. See—there is a clasp on the side."

Nathan popped the clasp up and opened the top. He quickly saw that it did not open from left to right or have pages as other books did. Turning it around and leaving the open part sticking up, he suddenly told the onlookers as lights came on inside, "This is a very, very strange book. Let's take it over there, Brinid, where we can see it better." Nathan began walking towards one of the nearby tables. He set the book down and waited as the rest of the group gathered around for a better view. The inside of the top was clear and lined with faint lights around it, while the bottom was lined with marked buttons and a few lights filling the rest of the inside. "May I please push the buttons, Chregg?" begged Nathan, ever eager to forge ahead.

It seemed that some of the buttons might make parts of words and that others contained whole words. Chregg nodded. Nathan pushed a button marked "Start." At once words appeared at the top saying, "This contains a copy of the Ancients' books. What would you like to read or study?"

"Oooooooh!" said Nathan the Bold. "I will come back to this later! I don't even know how to answer this first question; much less do I know what to do with a machine that will ask me more!" The group howled with laughter at their adventurous one's hesitation. "I guess we'd better read some of the other books first, huh?" he said closing the top. "Here, Brinid. You can put it up now," he said handing it back to her.

"Nathan's right, friends. Let's move on to the other case and look at the books there. First we can split among us the ones that we need most to skim. Richen, Borg and I will look through those that pertain to the weather. Brinid and Nathan, why don't you see if you can find something that will tell you how to work those strange books we just saw. Maybe try the one labeled "RECORDING DEVICES". Candra and Joden please take a look at the one that's labeled "HISTORY", and Jaren and Marland, if you would please look through the book that says "OPERATIONS AND EXPERIMENTS". We'll need to spread out to study. Candra, please see what is in those boxes on the tables there," he finished, pointing to the tables scattered around the area.

Candra took the lid off one of the boxes and found what must be very thin parchment. Not anything like their parchment that was thick and soft, but the group decided it was for writing. Searching further, she was able to find some sticks that would make marks without first dipping them. "The Dome people must have liked to write and study here," Candra observed. "Joden, if you could get our book, we can sit here." she called to her friend. "Whatever will we find?" she asked softly to no one in particular.

The others, finding their assigned books, began carrying them to tables or to the wide, soft chairs. "These next few days, we will skim and take notes on what we find, then make reports to each other," said Chregg as he sat on one of the wide chairs with Richen. Borg, facing them, sat on a stool. "May the One have His way," he encouraged with a smile.

Nathan echoed Chregg's blessing with a new version as he and Brinid took their seats at a table. "And, it is now 'soon'," he chuckled as everyone joined in for a laugh before getting serious.

CHAPTER SIX

A few days later having finished taking their notes and studying their assigned books and devices, the teams were now assembled in the meeting area. Each team waited anxiously, wanting to share what they had found. Chregg, who was a fair and orderly leader, set out the schedule for sharing. "Richen, Borg and I will talk about the rain problem first. Jaren and Marland will report what we need to know about operations. Candra and Joden will give us a brief history of the Dome and Atron and last but not least, our great recording devices experts, Nathan and Brinid, will share with us how to use the machines that ask questions." Candra and Joden were especially eager to share their discoveries. It was going to be all they could do to practice patience while the other teams talked. Their eyes brimming with excitement, they finally had to separate and quit looking at one another in order to be able to listen to the others' reports.

Richen began by summarizing the process they would need to go through to restore rain to their planet. "One of the objects we passed on our exploratory walk around the inside of the Dome is designed to regulate the planet's weather, by somehow regulating the air above and around the planet. The people of the Dome called them 'machines.' When the first people came to our planet, it was not quite livable for them. Atron was similar to their home planet, but lacked sufficient rain and wildlife. That is why the Dome was built. They were able to assemble the regulator machine with parts they had brought with them or were able to manufacture here on Atron. The book shows where we can find instructions that will help us reset and fine-tune this machine. It seems the Dome dwellers never meant for the Dome to go unvisited for so long. Once they were able to move out into the regulated air and weather, they still visited the Dome, studying the Ancient books, keeping the report books, watching over the regulator and doing experiments."

Borg continued their report. "A weather regulator that wasn't working precisely would not affect the Dome itself, but if it was left unadjusted, after a while it would begin to affect the atmosphere outside. The valued books and equipment that had traveled with them to Atron were left in the Dome for safekeeping. They named the regulator a 'MagnaRay' by the way," he added. "Some of the instructions are on recording devices with detailed descriptions, stored near the MagnaRay. Richen, Chregg and I will locate them tomorrow and begin to set into process the steps that should restore the rain. Don't you wish we could be there in Unidan and Tolden to see the people when the rain begins to fall after so long," he concluded with a grin. "That will be one happy day!"

"Alright. Jaren and Marland, what do we need to know about the operation of the Dome?" Chregg prompted the next sharers. Joden and Candra dared a look at each other, but they could not sustain it very long with such exciting news to share.

Smiling at the girls, Marland answered, "Some of what Richen and Chregg have already shared fits with our book. The Dome is made to be

 2006 Barbara Moon

completely self-sufficient and self-repairing as far as keeping the air, lights and anything to do with life-support running. The sun is the energy source and the roof of the dome serves as the collection point for all the energy generated from here. This is what is happening when we see the various colors bouncing around above it. As we already know, the sun shines most of the time during the day providing an endless source of energy. The knowledge of how to do this that our ancestors brought with them is beyond my understanding, but it is truly remarkable."

"I certainly do not understand how they can make food from a machine that no food is put into, but they do it," continued Jaren scratching her head and smiling. I understand how to hunt and how to cook on a fire, and that's about all I can say about getting food," she added. "The water supply seems to be connected to something underground and then is cleaned and reused over and over. It should not run out for hundreds and hundreds of years."

"Thanks, Scouts," Chregg said. "And now let's hear from our lovely historians who are about to burst with their news."

Candra and Joden treated their audience to a bow as they laughed at Chregg's introduction, releasing some of their pent up anticipation. "We the historians will need more than one session to give a full report," a grinning Candra began. "The report book is like a journal with the leaders of each generation making regular entries, more like a story. The other book we looked at today starts at the beginning." Candra paused to sort her thoughts, wanting to keep the best for last. "Many, many years ago the people who built this Dome lived on another planet, far from Atron, perhaps a star we can see in our night sky. Many of the people on that planet, greatly corrupted by evil leaders, had forgotten The One of the Ancients. An advanced society, they used their machines and inventions to travel through space. It was a common thing for these people to explore the skies."

Taking another deep breath, Candra continued her tale, "Some families, who had not followed the evil ways, banded together. Deeply concerned for their children's future with The One, they feared their faith would die out if something drastic did not occur. They suffered and struggled for many years, hoping to bring back the ancient beliefs of our faith. They never forgot or turned their backs on The One. But no matter how hard they tried to explain their faith in The One, the people around them refused to listen to anything they had to say and instead chose to rely on themselves and their inventions, turning even further from The One. Finally, the little band of families felt that they had to leave and find another place to live so that their children could grow up knowing and being blessed by their ancient beliefs. Several of them, familiar with the machines and marvels of their planet, were experienced with traveling into space. After much study, the group collected, planned and prepared to take their families to a planet they believed would sustain life if assisted by their machines. Those families were our ancestors who came here to Atron. And we are their descendants!" Finished with her part of their story, Candra paused for a breath, smiled, and then nodded at Joden.

Joden took up the tale where Candra had left off. "They landed on this planet which they named Atron in honor of their leaders who had brought them to this planet. This first group of settlers lived inside their ships, working outside only after they put on special suits, until the Dome was finished. Later on, they moved into the Dome until the planet became completely habitable. Collected inside here is most of the knowledge and equipment they brought with them. Their civilization had already advanced to levels we haven't even begun to understand."

Now Joden's tone changed from serious to joy-filled and Candra's face lit up almost as brightly as the electrokey as Joden continued. Finally the best news came bubbling out, "But most of all, they saved the Ancients' Books! These are copies of the ones that came directly from the first writers for The One. Our book says He 'breathed on the first writers and they wrote His words through the Spirit of The One.' After reading, we can say that it's clear that all of what Gran has taught us is true. Our One is the same One they speak of in their writings."

Candra could sit still no longer. She stood up and continued the story. "Those crazy books that Nathan opened contain the Ancients' books, The One's books. The people of the Dome put them on those special devices so everyone could read and study them and so they would be preserved! We can read them for ourselves!"

"And," Joden added, "They preserved one of the ancient books bound in leather just as it had been in the days they were written! It is in a special case!" Everyone grew quiet allowing a few moments for this last bit of news to sink in. But then the air was filled with their excited chatter, punctuated by great smiles and hugs.

"We can read The One's books?"

"They are right here in the Dome like we were taught?"

"The Toldens will have to believe now!"

"I can't wait to tell Gran!"

Chregg waited while this newest celebration faded once again to quiet. Then he said strongly, his voice filled with emotion, "We are truly the most blessed people. Now let's continue with the reports from these wonderful historians who have somehow managed to keep this to themselves all morning without the first, 'Whooooeeeee!'"

Candra picked up the story. "Once the machines finished their jobs and our planet became livable, our ancestors decided to move out of the Dome and build their new lives. The plants and wildlife had grown into great forests and meadows, with lovely streams flowing through them, as the weather regulator continued to do its work. The animals we hunt came with them from their home planet. Through experiments conducted here at the Dome, the people learned ways to help the animals become hearty, so that they could become a plentiful source of food and clothing for the young colony. Our ancestors wanted a new beginning using as few machines as possible outside the Dome. According to the journals, the mountain where we found the electrokey is the same now as it was then except for the vegetation that began to grow up its sides after the MagnaRay began working. The rains brought by the machines, purified the water in the pond. In the journals they talk about the way the water turns colors when the sun strikes the pond. It was that way when they first found it, created by the The One.

The Tazors we have are the same ones they had in their time. The families lived in peace, so they were seldom used. Our ancestors, now free to live together in the ways of The One, immersed themselves in the tasks of growing, enjoying and working in their new world." Suddenly Candra's glowing face grew sad and quiet as she glanced over to Joden. Joden's voice reflected Candra's sadness, as she took up the tale.

"As we know, something happened to split apart those original settlers' descendants. I think we'll have to read more of the report books to get all the details. And, I want to get the time-line straight, too. So is it all right, Chregg, if we finish our report later? We would like to spend today thinking about what we've already read."

"Surely, Joden," answered Chregg. Looking around the circle at each Participant he added, "Do we want to hear the last report now or save it for later?"

"Now! Now!" Nathan eagerly cast votes for both himself and Brinid. The others lightheartedly agreed, so he began. "The girls are right! The crazy book, as the girls called it and the ones from the case beside the door are the Ancients' books that have been put into the machines. We can look up any part of them, any time we want. We can ask questions and get answers. The books will help us study by asking us questions to help us learn, along with The One, of course. The Ancients' book, given by The One, has always been called 'one book', though it is made up of many books. These books also house other books about the Ancients and their writings about The One. If we want to look at The One's book, we can push buttons inside the cover and it will give us a list of the books it houses within. Each of the study books is identical. They are powered by the sun."

Finished, Nathan turned to Brinid and she gladly continued their report, "These machine books are only one kind of recording device that the settlers brought with them. There are all sizes of them and they are what run most of the Dome. Some of the other devices show pictures that move or allow us to listen to voices and sounds. Our book tells us how to work them all, when we have the time to figure it out." She concluded with a sigh, "Learning all these new things is making me very tired."

"This is truly too much to take in all at once," Chregg voiced, and the others nodded agreement. "Let's stop our reports here for the night, take time to rest, and then continue our work tomorrow.

CHAPTER SEVEN

Five more days passed quickly as the adventurers continued to check out the Dome. Nathan and Brinid combed the book that explained the recording devices, finally deciphering how to work most of the ones they needed. The time they spent exploring the new books had drawn Nathan and Brinid closer each day. Nathan, still quite young to think about committing to another as his Last Companion, could not seem to stop his growing love for Brinid. The longer she walked with The One, the more evident it became that she was changing. Her face, once troubled by fear and shame, now reflected the peace and trust she had found by relaxing in The One's love and care for her. Like the Ancients' teachings said, *The Love of the One will heal and set free anyone who decides to follow Him.* Occasionally Nathan and Brinid talked about The One's love and their growing love for each other. Brinid felt drawn to Nathan. They decided they wanted it to keep growing, and that they would talk more with Father and Gran about it after they returned to Unidan. For now they would concentrate on exploring the Dome and keep their vows of purity, a commitment expected to be honored by all who followed The One. Being together and learning more about each other and how they related together would be enough for now.

Exploring the Dome together was a good time for Candra to speak with Joden, Marland, Jaren or Brinid about her love for Eric and how much she missed him. Dreaming about the future, the five women, giggling in their cubicle after studies and meals discussed in detail what Candra's ceremony to become a Last Companion might be like. "Is it not just like The One to bring them together-- the two future leaders of our world?" They marveled to each other over and over. Candra's hopes grew each day as she thought about how the love she and Eric shared might be a part of the completion of The Cause Gran had so often talked with her about.

Candra also grew to love Brinid more and more as she listened to Brinid share about her past life and how difficult it had been. Candra wanted Brinid to understand how happy they all were to have her with them, and not just because she had given them the parchment. Never wanting to miss a chance, she often found herself saying, "Brinid, we all love you so much for just being who you are." These healing words would sink deep inside Brinid's heart and her eyes would shine back to everyone how much those words meant.

Like the other explorers, Chregg and Richen had carefully studied both written and recorded words to find instructions for using the MagnaRay correctly. Today, they were ready to reset the MagnaRay to its original specifications designed to bring periodic rain to the thirsty planet. Crowding around the huge machine, everyone watched the two men as they entered the complex sequence of switches that would start the process of resetting the weather patterns. "All is prepared, Chregg," prompted Richen as he kept a watchful eye on all the lights and buttons. "You can punch in that last code when you're ready."

Chregg paused for a moment to check inside with The One and then punched in the correct sequence of numbers and letters and then hit the "Reset" button. The ever present clanking noise the travelers had grown accustomed to hearing from the Magna Ray changed instantly into a soft whir. They watched now as a brilliant purple ray pierced the Dome's cover and instantly shot straight up into the sky. The purple ray disappeared into Atron's cloud cover and then became invisible as the Magna Ray's soft whir slowly diminished until they could barely hear a sound. Checking the panel of lights and switches, Chregg and Richen assured the others that all was well. "Let's go outside and watch!" Chregg suggested expectantly and everyone moved outside the Dome to see what might happen next.

The clouds began to pick up speed, seeming to billow and grow as if large hands were scooping them together. The sky, quickly darkening from blue to gray for as far as the eye could see, soon covered the sun with a mass of thick clouds. As the first drops of rain they had seen or felt in over a year splashed happily onto their upturned faces, cheers went up all around as everyone danced and splashed in the puddles growing at their feet.

Soon a loud rumbling from the sky joined the cheers and shortened the celebration dance, as the first peals of thunder heard on Atron in quite a while boomed from cloud to cloud. As the wind began fiercely blowing the trees' branches back and forth, they witnessed the first bolt of lightning streak quickly from sky to land. "We'd better get back inside," Chregg yelled, laughing in spite of the danger. "This storm might be great, making up for what has been lost. We will come back outside after it passes," Chregg assured the young people as they scooted through the doorway and into the Dome. "This storm serves well as a sign to everyone in Unidan and those in Tolden who know about us, to tell them we are here and safe. Atron is saved! Thank You, Our One!"

# # # #

And--at that very moment in Tolden, Eric heard the unmistakable sounds of a storm brewing and bent his knees to thank The One as well. He was grateful first for the rain and then that this meant that, hopefully, his beloved was among those new friends who had made it safely to the Dome.

# # # #

In Unidan, Gran, Handen, Esleda and their people also bowed before their King, thanking Him for the same. What wonderful news this storm brought! Those they had not seen for almost three weeks had succeeded in finding the Dome and bringing the much-needed rain.

CHAPTER EIGHT

The next day a happy group of explorers gathered in the study area seated around tables with one of Nathan's "crazy books" in front of them. He and Brinid had spent much of their time in the Dome learning how to operate the different types of recording devices. "Now," Nathan projected in his best teaching voice, "Brinid and I will show you how to use these special books. We will be able to carry a couple of these back with us to our people so they will be able to read the book of The One for themselves. Most of the other devices must remain here in order to be used. But Borg will talk more about that later," he added glancing at Borg with his irrepressible grin.

Nathan and Brinid then proceeded to show the excited explorers how they could make these books work. Once equipped, no one wanted to leave the study area for a long time, amazed at all the writings that confirmed and expanded many of the things that they'd been taught all their lives.

Later that evening as they sat in the meeting area and listened to the lovely raindrops beating on the roof of the Dome, Candra and Joden told Chregg that they felt they were ready to talk more about the history of their ancestors. "We have the time-line straightened out fairly well," began Joden. "I worked it out as best I could from knowing what Gran has taught us all, and using the entries from the journal-like books. This will be a little confusing with all the 'Greats' so bear with us as you listen. First let's review the ones we know about and bring Brinid better up to date since she doesn't know all the names. Candra, please recite the lineage for us," Joden said.

"First we will start with me, next in line for leader of our people," said Candra humbly. "As you know, before me is my Father, Handen. Gran is his mother, married to Wilden. Gran's mother was named Sandlen, married to Jazen. Gran's mother's father was Kolen, married to Elezaban. Next, the Father of Kolen was Damond, son of Vandlyn. Vandlyn was the king who was killed by his friend. His son Damond was the man who signed the big book we first read and the one who hid the parchment after his father was killed. So Gran's great, great grandfather was Damond, one of the two who split the parchment in half. Now you go ahead, Joden," she prompted with a touch on Joden's sleeve.

Smiling at the group, Joden said, "I told you there were lots of 'greats', especially if we said it from Candra all the way back to the beginning. By getting the line of succession straight, I was able to figure out that the splitting of the parchment was around 175 seasons ago. The original Dome people did not have kings, but somewhere in the years before the split, two leaders were chosen and sometimes called kings. They agreed to lead together. As best I've been able to discover, something about the experiments that were going on in the Dome caused a big disagreement between the two leaders. It seems that the one we are calling the 'bad king,' Brasald, was secretly doing unauthorized experiments in the Dome. Candra and I think this is what accounts for the huge animals, flowers and vines that we've already seen on our journey. When Vandlyn found out about the experiments, this caused a split between the two peoples. To preserve things as they were and to prevent any further experiments, Vandlyn locked the Dome. He hoped that, at the worst, his son, Damond ,would return to the Dome after convincing the others to put an end to the dangerous experiments. He hoped this would happen within his son's generation.

We can surmise from what we heard from Gran and Lornen that this didn't happen, and the two sides grew still further apart after the parchment was split and the Dome was lost to both." Joden sat quietly allowing the others a moment to catch up. Quietly, each Participant pondered the story and then committed it to heart. After a short time, Joden spoke aloud to The One.

"Oh, One, our King, we thank You for showing us the past more clearly. We ask You, as The One, to guide us in these times, so that unity may be restored to the peoples of Atron. Help us learn how to keep such divisions from happening again. Keep these stories fresh in our minds, that the power here in the Dome may be only used as You lead." As Joden finished her plea, the rest looked up at her, their eyes mirroring back a look of determination.

As the group sat quietly together, thinking through all they had learned these last few weeks, Chregg spoke to his fellow Participants. "As soon as the rain stops we will leave the Dome and return to Unidan and Tolden. The MagnaRay is working again and we believe that the rain will soak the land for this cycle. Tonight we will decide which things we will take back with us. We will take only those things that will best serve The Cause to reunite our people. Scouts, we will need you to hunt and prepare supplies so that we may be ready to travel with sunlight the day after the rain ends. We can take some of the Dome food with us as well. And we must stay alert for the dangerous plants and animals. I don't want to lose anymore people."

CHAPTER NINE

With rain falling on the fields of Tolden, Eric felt relief as he thought about how he would feed his own people and also those of Unidan. Most of the people in the city had danced in the streets, splashing in and celebrating the three-day downpour. They watched as fields and forests grew greener and streams rippled with rushing water instead of the trickles they had grown accustomed to. The rains had been so strong that it seemed like the river was rising even as they watched. Though he had not brought the rain with him, Eric knew that the city was very different since his return. It warmed his heart to know that though Tylina had not lived to see it, she had not dreamed of change in vain. Nor had his mother. Nor Brinid's parents' hopes, with their longing for a better Tolden, been in vain. Now through these faithful one's children, real change had come.

Now that Eric had a solid backing of followers who were helping him bring changes to the people of Tolden, he was able to spread the news that, instead of just rumors, The One is actually real, that the old rumors about His goodness and power, heard throughout Tolden, were really the truth. The new guards, who walked the perimeter, were no longer trying to keep Toldens in and Unidans out but instead watched for things that would upset the peace that had begun to spread throughout the city. They also helped to round up those who were not happy with Eric's changes.

As Eric made decrees allowing the Unidans to live freely among the Toldens, a steady stream of people from the camp came to relieve or help their friends who worked in the fields. The Unidan people in Tolden began cautiously sharing the great love put into their hearts by The One, and it became easier for the people of Tolden to begin working alongside them as brothers instead of enemies, helping to grow the grain needed to feed both peoples. The much-needed rain greatly aided their labor, as much as the lifestyle of kindness and joy that the Unidans had always lived and now shared with their Tolden friends. Joy spread and grew around the city as citizens of both Unidan and Tolden worked together to make changes that would help the city become a cleaner, better place to live, bringing hope to the Toldens.

Aids and advisors worked on the problem of the city children who had been running wildly in the streets. Classes were slowly improving as Unidan elders helped set up teaching time that encouraged children to attend class more often. And with the promise of work and better provisions for food, parents had less pressure and were beginning to take better care of their children. All over the city, all those who had already known The One and who were coming to know Him in this new environment of freedom, were encouraged to spread His love to others--and this new way of thinking and being was working. Families found themselves agreeing to take children, who like Brinid, had been living in the streets, eating garbage and stealing in order to survive, into their homes. Much of the old wariness the people of the city and camp had felt towards each other began to slowly die away as they worked together and got to know each other better. Reminding himself that it would take a long time to develop full peace and unity, Eric felt greatly encouraged as he saw hope springing up in the hearts of people all around him.

Though the kings before him had used scribes to keep a log of their activities, Eric had decided to write his own in addition to the official logs. These writings were personal and not only spoke of all the changes that were taking place in the city, but spoke also of the changes in him as he learned more of The One. Tonight he wrote:

> *How well I remember that first time I went to Unidan after I returned and asked Handen if he and Esleda, Lornen and Gran would come to our city to meet with us. With the advisors and old followers from my mother's time who had come forward to help, it seemed there might be a possibility of getting our two peoples together. We all spent much time talking with The One before undertaking such an event.*

> *In our first meeting, the Unidans made it clear to us that they did not want a king. Since knowing their ways and love for The One, I understood. We discussed ways we could make an easy transition away from having a king as peace began to take hold in Tolden. After much*

talk, it was decided that having a king right now to back up changes and new decrees would be an advantage as a show of visible power during the adjustment period. And as the Unidan leaders and I'd hoped, this meeting went fairly well, with the Unidans winning everyone over with their love and kindness. I greatly enjoyed how Handen stilled some of my people's doubts with his gentle strength. The way he handled the meeting had the opposite effect of my father's bellowing and selfishness. Instead of fear and anger, our people responded to him with growing trust and respect. We thanked The One for His ways within and through us. Now it is easier to see how the people will accept my beloved Candra when she returns from her mission at the Dome. What a day of celebration it will be for all of us when the time comes for us to be joined as Last Companions!

Eric pictured Candra's face, smiling as he remembered one of the talks they'd had together. Lately, he found himself smiling often as he recalled their many talks that had taken place while he was recuperating in Unidan. *I am so amazed at how The One has brought us together and all that is unfolding in His plan for us. I can hardly wait to see her face again,* he thought filled with anticipation. *Dare I begin to look for their return soon now that the rains have come? If the Unidans agree, perhaps we will send out a party of trustworthy scouts to intercept them. That would mean having to copy the parchment map and directions again.* "Hummm," Eric mumbled under his breath as he turned to his aide, "Send word to the Unidan leaders that I wish another meeting." As his aide moved toward the door, he thought better and called the aide back to his side, "Better yet," he said, "I will go to Unidan myself."

CHAPTER TEN

From among Eric's trustworthy men and Handen's young Participants who were eager to go and meet the Dome travelers, they selected a group of eight. Setting out the next day with a new map in hand, they followed the same northeasterly direction that the first party had taken. The first few days went by without incidence, but on their sixth day, they heard a sharp sound that could only be Tazor fire.

Breaking into a run, the eight hurried towards the sounds, greatly concerned for their friends. They broke from the forest at a run, just in time to see a huge furry creature, with its back to them, blocking their way. On each side, two other creatures stood equally large and threatening. Quickly assessing the situation, they could see that another beast was down on the ground, lying on its side, its fur smoking from a fatal Tazor wound. Inching their way forward, they noticed that the stench coming from the beasts was so over powering it was nauseating. Carefully moving to where they could peek between the large creatures, the ones in front could see that the very adventurers they had been hoping to intercept were backed against a large mound of rocks. "Raise Tazors and set to kill," the lead Tolden from Eric's mission quickly ordered. "Target each of the animals, firing at will." The Dome travelers, not expecting more than one creature at a time, realized that their combined Tazor power had only been able to kill one of the animals. Hearing the command shouted from behind the beasts, the original party thanked the One for sending a rescue party and then raised their Tazors a second time to fire at the creatures. This time the combined power of the Tazor fire was enough, and soon all five of the creatures began to wobble, and mortally wounded, slowly topple over, crashing to the ground. The

2006 Barbara Moon

returning Dome travelers sank to their knees in relief, while the newly arrived rescuers checked the area for additional threats. Soon the rescue party was greeting their friends from the Dome with a round of hugs and introductions.

With great excitement they exchanged stories, first the rescuing party told of all the changes that had been taking place in Tolden, then those who had been returning from the Dome shared some of their discoveries from their time at the Dome. "What a sight to see you together," Candra blurted out to the Toldens. "Thank you first for saving us, but also thanks to The One for sending you to us at the right time. And," she added, "for His work that has obviously happened among our peoples that you would come together." Addressing her question to anyone who could answer, she asked shyly, "How is Eric?"

"A most marvelous and wise leader," One of the Toldens answered. "There are so many things you will need to see to believe," he continued.

"It was his idea to send us to join you," added one of the others. "We are four days out from Unidan. Soon you all will be able to see the progress that's going on for yourselves."

Another Tolden stepped forward, "If we are agreed, let's send two people from our party to travel back to Tolden as fast as possible. They will report that we have found you and give them a time that you should arrive in the city. What do you think?"

Clapping his new comrade on the back, Chregg said, "That is a great idea. I think we can manage much better with your additional help and still spare two of you to go on ahead. In addition to meeting up with these beasts, we almost lost another of our friends to a huge vine as we made our way back from the Dome. And because he is wounded, traveling has been slower." Looking around at the others, Chregg continued, "But if I remember correctly, we did not encounter any of the large creatures on our trip to the Dome, before reaching these rocks. Is that what you others remember?"

The other scouts nodded in assent. Richen added, "Once we get back to the city, hunting down and destroying any other changed animals and plants will need to be one of our first missions in order to assure safe travel back and forth to the Dome."

"That is certain," Chregg agreed for all. Nodding to the Tolden scout, he finished, "Do you want to start back?"

"We two will begin now," said the Tolden as he pointed questioningly to one of the Unidans to join him. The other nodded his assent and the two turned to leave. "We'll see you in the city."

"May The One have His Way," the others called in blessing as they waved goodbye, "and protect you as you go."

The two soon disappeared back into the dense forest they had so recently come out of to help the travelers. Chregg motioned for everyone to gather around. "Let's rest for a while and then we'll cover more ground ourselves before nightfall."

"Let's first move away from these beasts," Nathan said holding his nose. "They smell horrible. I hope the sun takes care of them before we come back or they'll smell even worse." Following his suggestion, the newly formed party moved further into the leafy cover of the forest and rested before starting home. During this respite, they took the time to fill each other in on all the wonderful things that The One had been doing, at the Dome and in the city.

CHAPTER ELEVEN

It had been two days since the scouts' quick and safe return to report that the Dome party was on its way to Tolden. Unidans came to help the city prepare a celebration in honor their return. Colorful banners proclaiming "Welcome" hung all over the city. A huge feast was being prepared as everyone contributed what he could. Musicians tuned their instruments while children practiced songs and dances. Nothing was left out, as they made plans for a great time of rejoicing over the returning adventurers. News of the discoveries that had been made at the Dome helped more and more people forget the divisions that had existed among them. Dissenters and grumblers felt so outnumbered that they finally gave up their complaints and decided to stay inside.

Watching the jubilation below from his balcony, Eric sighed with contentment. *This truly is a most remarkable day. We celebrate the rain that brings food to our people. We celebrate our two peoples coming together under the One. And I will see Candra again. Will she be different? Will she still love me? Will she like the changes we've made? Not to worry*, Eric reminded himself. *The One is who I trust!*

"I see them! I see them! I see them!" the cry grew louder as it moved from the crowded outskirts to the very center of the city. Instantly, Eric's heart began to race with anticipation. "They're here! They're here! There they are!" He heard as the shouts continued to rise and float along the streets.

His eyes searched the crowded streets, until suddenly Eric's love emerged from a large group of people as the traveling party made their way closer to the castle. Her cloak was torn and filthy, her boots in tatters, yet she was smiling through the tears that streaked her lovely face. Tied at the end with a scraggly piece of cloth, her braid hung loosely down her back, and Eric thought, *I have never seen anything so beautiful in my life.* He found himself running down the castle steps to join the parade as it neared the castle. As the crowd parted to make a path for him, Candra caught her first glimpse of Eric. There in front of her people and his, many of whom had never seen her before, Candra broke into a run aimed directly for his arms. Reaching her destination, she hugged him so tightly Eric could hardly breathe. "I missed you so much," she cried with joy. "'I've missed you so much!"

It became very clear from such a show of affection, that Candra must be the one who would become their leader alongside Eric. The cheers increased as the two, oblivious to the commotion around them, clung to one another, alternating between kisses, hugs and loving looks into each other's eyes. Gran, Handen and Esleda soon joined the greeting as well, showering each returning traveler with cries of joy, so grateful for their safe return. They could hardly contain their excitement in waiting to hear all about the marvels and tales from the journey to the great Dome of their ancestors.

This walk of celebration through the city streets soon ended as the adventurers turned toward the castle, entering its great hall surrounded by their families and closest friends. They dined and rested, enjoying the company and comforts of home. It would take many days to tell the stories and share the many wonders they had discovered at the Dome. That was fine with the people of Unidan and Tolden, because they somehow knew that this new king and his wonderful new Companion would lead them with grace and love. The true *Unidan* King, The One Within, was in them both, giving them His guidance and assurance that all the marvels that had been uncovered at the lost Dome of Atron would serve His people well.

Epilogue

Candra and Joden, alone in one of the small rooms in the castle at
Tolden, whispered and giggled as if they were still children sitting in a class
with the Elders. Bright sunlight streaming through a large window gave
enough light for the girls to see without a lamp. Along one wall a long table
sat piled high with flowers of every color. Some had been woven into
bouquets, while others lay scattered across the table and onto the floor. On
the opposite wall, a protruding hook held a lovely dress of indescribable
material and color.

"Can you believe today is the day, Candra, when you and Eric will be
joined forever?" Joden asked as she brushed Candra's long unbraided hair.
"You wondered if it would ever come, didn't you?"

"Right after my Becoming Day, I did wonder if I would have such a day
as this," her radiant friend replied happily. "Just look at this dress. Even
more look at my face! I have so much joy inside that the dress pales in
comparison. I feel like dancing or pacing, but it's time for me to put on my
Joining dress. Joden, you have to help me stay calm. It's difficult!"

"Out shining such a dress as this is difficult, too," Joden teased as she
took the dress from its hook and helped Candra pull it carefully over her
head. "Your mother and Gran have outdone themselves with the piece of
cloth that Eric found here in one of the castle trunks. It is hard to find words
to describe how it shimmers and glows--almost like the colors that bounce
off the Dome. You truly look like a queen--and your face definitely does
show it," Joden agreed as she lifted Candra's hair so she could hook the back

2006 Barbara Moon

of her dress. The top of the dress had delicately stitched flowers scattered all across the front of it. Gran and Esleda had carefully stitched each flower, combining threads of various shades from their color pots. These lacey flowers matched the real ones from Candra's headpiece and bouquet that were now resting on the table, woven together by loving hands. The skirt, full and flowing, fell towards the floor until it just brushed the tops of new white boots made especially for Candra by Lornen. As Joden said, the color and material of the dress were like nothing the Unidans had ever seen. The cloth, made from a different kind of plant than the Unidans had access to, was shiny and reflective, its hues reflecting the changes in sunlight, lamplight or candlelight.

"I know that we are to enjoy our beauty from within, from The One," Candra said to her best friend, "but isn't it fun to look so lovely on the outside? I thank The One for all of it."

With a knock on the door, Esleda interrupted their conversation as she peeked around the door to see if she could enter. Esleda and Gran were here to help with the final preparations before Candra would walk out to the Great Hall to be joined with her Last Companion. Handen was standing with Eric behind the Hall, waiting for the instruments to begin playing as they signaled the entrance of the new queen.

"Come in, Mother," Candra beckoned with a big smile. "Is Gran with you?"

"I would not miss this time for anything," chimed in Gran as she followed Esleda inside the double doors. Both mothers gave a kiss to Candra and a hug to Joden. "To be joined with a Last Companion is one of our most precious traditions," continued Gran. "And only a few are allowed to see the bride before the ceremony. Your mother and I have the privilege of escorting you to Eric, along with Joden--your best friend, of course. How are you two staying so calm?"

"It is all Candra can do to refrain from dancing in her joy," laughed Joden. "She has asked me to hold her down."

"This is such a beautiful dress, Mother--and Gran, and I am so excited to be joining with the Last Companion that The One has brought me! I will have to dance eventually or I will burst."

"Not to mention that he is very handsome," Joden grinned as she turned to pick up the flowers that would circle Candra's head.

Esleda took the flowers, woven together like a crown, from Joden's hands and placed them on her daughter's head. She then leaned over to the nearby stool and picked up Candra's bouquet. Nearly every color of flower that grew on Atron was in the headpiece and the bouquet, coordinating with the ones so lovingly stitched on the Joining dress. Reds, pinks, yellows and purples intermingled with tiny specks of orange, white and green throughout the pieces. As she handed the bouquet to Candra, Esleda spoke the ancient blessing of their people: "May The One have His Way." Candra swallowed back tears as she took the flowers from her mother.

Softy touching her granddaughter's shoulder, Gran spoke to The One about this very special day. "Dear One, How grateful we are for Your guidance and love. We stand here today knowing that Your hand has brought these two together and that Your grace has made it possible for Atron to be saved and brought to peace. May Your ways continue to grow here in Tolden as Eric and Candra seek You to lead through them. We Elders commit ourselves to continue supporting and guiding them as Your ways spread among the people and they come to know You as You truly are. I thank you for the ceremony that is to come and the joyful dancing that will follow. It is in Your Presence and through Your very Life within us that we do all that we do."

The four women smiled gently at each other as they raised their eyes. Gran bent to fluff Candra's dress one more time and Esleda opened the door. Joden walked quickly ahead of Candra to signal the players of the instruments. Nearing the door of the Great Hall, Candra smelled the candles and the flowers that her friends and family had brought with them to decorate the Hall. The tapestries had been changed and rewoven to honor The One instead of the evil king. Candra listened as the harpists begin to strum the Joining song. The melody flowed throughout the Hall and passed through the open balconies where people gathered in the streets could hear. Chimes rang softly, and muted drums joined with the harps to make a delicate melody. Inside the Great Hall, all eyes were turned to the door in the back of the hall through which Candra would enter.

Eric, Handen, and Nathan waited at the front of the Great Hall. Brinid sat in the front row of stools along with the other Participants who had traveled to the Dome. As Candra stepped through the door, Eric stood spellbound, watching as her dress reflected the candlelight, her face aglow with joy. She smiled at him and began to walk between the rows of friends and family, Esleda on one side, Gran on the other. Joden came behind her to complete the symbolic circle of love that would surround Candra as Eric took her hand.

Candra still wanting to dance, asked The One Within to be her calm. She smiled, looking into the eyes of her Last Companion as she stood before him. Taking his hand, she then turned with Eric to face Handen. His words would soon allow them to become one. Esleda, Gran and Joden stood next to Nathan as Handen began the ceremony by speaking to the people in the Great Hall. "People of Atron, you see here the young people whom The One has called together to reunite us. He has brought the rain to save our world. He has shown us the Dome of old and allowed us to find His Books that were lost. This Joining becomes for us the symbol of a new beginning, not unlike the one that brought the Ancients here to Atron. These two will have much work to do, leading our peoples and continuing the repairs needed from years of fighting. We that know The One will trust Him as we do all that can be done to help resettle our world."

Turning to the couple, Handen smiled at them and asked, "Eric and Candra, do you pledge as Last Companions to remain true only to each other and The One; to ask for help when struggles threaten to overcome you; to keep the Words of The One and follow Him in all things; to teach your children His ways; and to speak the truth in openness, love and honesty to one another?"

Eric was first to respond. "Candra, Now <u>My</u> Beloved One, I pledge these things to you, as your father and The One have said." Eric's eyes lit up and his smile was contagious as he awaited his beloved's response.

"Eric, ever my Companion, I pledge these things to you as my father and The One have said," echoed Candra with an equally contagious smile. *If my father does not hurry, the dancing is going to begin before the ceremony ends and the music resumes,* Candra thought to herself, her feet tapping under the flowing dress. Joden chuckled softly and sneaked a glance at Brinid who was also about to laugh. They could see Candra's feet moving, as their friend was barely able to contain her joy.

At last Handen said the final words, "You are joined for life, until the presence of The One is no longer within, but face to face." Remembering Eric's question at their first pledge to one another, Handen laughingly said, "And now Eric you may kiss your Companion with permission from the witnesses. Then let the dancing begin!"

And so Eric did.

And finally Candra danced!

Made in the USA
Columbia, SC
13 February 2025

53794610R00120